Chloe Chang—Superstar?

Suddenly I became aware of a strange sound. With a jolt, I realized what it was. Voices were chanting my name over and over.

I turned sharply. Behind me, about thirty kids were being held in back of a barricade by zoo security. "Chloe! Chloe!" they chanted. When they saw I was looking at them, they started waving autograph books. "Chloe, sign my book." "Chloe, sign my hand!" "Sign my T-shirt!"

I went over to the kids and began signing stuff. "We love you, Chloe!" called a girl. Behind her, two other girls waved their autograph books at me. "We do, we love you!" they shouted.

How could they love me? They didn't even know me.

Chloe mania was getting really crazy!

Cover
Kids

Chloe Mania!

Suzanne Weyn

Troll Associates

For Shanafe Stovall, with love

LIBRARY OF CONGRESS CATALOGING-IN-PUBLICATION DATA

Weyn, Suzanne.
    Chloe mania! / by Suzanne Weyn.
        p.   cm. — (Cover kids)
    Summary: Thirteen-year-old Chloe Chang manages to balance
modeling, school, and work in her family's restaurant, but when she
receives an offer to work on a popular television series, she is not
sure that she wants to be a celebrity.
    ISBN 0-8167-3233-7 (lib.)   ISBN 0-8167-3234-5 (pbk.)
    [1. Models (Persons)—Fiction.   2. Chinese Americans—Fiction
    3. Fame—Fiction.]   I. Title.   II. Series.
PZ7.W539Cj   1994
[Fic]—dc20   93-42853

A TROLL BOOK, published by Troll Associates.

Chloe Mania!

Chapter One

———◆———

All right, Chloe," said the photographer who had his camera trained on me. "Turn around and look over your shoulder. I want to show the bow on the back of this dress."

I turned toward the large roll of blue paper that formed the backdrop for the picture. With my hands on my hips, I looked back at the photographer, who was named Sam. I smiled brightly for a moment and then faced front again.

Sam didn't tell me to stop, so I struck another pose, tilting my head to the side and pouting. Then I lifted my chin and shielded my eyes with my hand, as if I was looking at something off in the distance.

"Excellent!" said Sam as he continued taking pictures.

"You really know how to make the shots interesting, Chloe."

"Thanks," I said. I should know what I'm doing by now, I thought. Although I turned thirteen just last week, I've been a model for nine years.

When I was four, everyone told my mother I should be a model. I guess I was pretty cute. And people told her I had a lot of personality. They also told her the money would be great. So she brought me down to the Calico Modeling Agency.

The people at the agency liked me right away. Within a week, I appeared in an ad for a kids' cereal. The picture of me eating cereal and talking to a big pink cartoon bunny was everywhere. From then on, the modeling jobs just never stopped coming.

"Chloe, try on that blue checked dress, okay?" said Sam.

"Sure," I said, picking the dress off a clothes rack. I was about to go into the changing room when I saw a tall, gorgeous woman with short brown hair enter the studio. It was Kate Calico, head of the Calico Modeling Agency. She had stopped in at the agency's in-house photo studio to see how things were going.

Kate is so stylish. Today she had on a mint-green spring suit with a creamy, off-white top and cream-colored shoes. Kate always looks perfect. She's also extremely charming.

"Hello, Sam. How are things going?" she greeted the photographer.

"When you send me Chloe Chang, everything goes smoothly," Sam said with a smile. "What other girls do you have lined up for me to shoot?"

Kate smiled and waved to me as she told him the names of the other models she'd selected to be in the Little Princess clothing catalog. One of them was my best friend, Ashley Taylor. She was scheduled to come in the next morning.

Like me, Ashley has been a model since she was little. Ashley actually started when she was a baby. We have a lot in common. We both live in the city, we're both models, and we're the same age. But we're also pretty different.

Ashley is tall and has long, naturally wavy blond hair. I'm just five-feet-one, and I have short black hair.

Ashley lives uptown in a super fancy apartment with a doorman and everything. Her mother is a famous talk show host, and her dad is a TV director in California. (Her parents are divorced.) Even her older brother Johnny is a famous TV star. Ashley's got a live-in housekeeper named Katya. She also has a tutor, so she doesn't have to go to regular school.

I live downtown on top of my family's restaurant in the Chinatown section of the city. I'm in the eighth grade at Harriet Tubman Junior High. I have two sisters and three brothers (none of them famous). And my grandparents on my mom's side live in the apartment above ours.

Despite our differences, Ashley and I are best friends. We are also close with two other models, Nikki Wilton and Tracey Morris. They live out in the suburbs, but they come into the city to model.

"Chloe, I hear you're doing wonderfully," said Kate. "Sam is really pleased with your work. There's so much work for models in catalogs these days. You're just a natural for catalog work."

I knew why she was speaking to me about catalog work—because I'm a shrimp!

I suppose I should explain. You see, at thirteen, models are making the change from being kid models to being real adult models. Of course, depending on how old you look, you might have a year or two more of being a kid model. I've been told I look young for my age, so I can probably stretch things awhile longer.

When you're a kid, you don't have to be gorgeous and tall. You just have to be cute. But if you want to keep modeling through your teens and into adulthood, then you have to grow up to be tall—which I'm definitely not! About the only jobs for short models are modeling petite clothing in catalogs.

Catalog work is okay. Sometimes you even go someplace nice like Hawaii or England so that they can get interesting backgrounds in the pictures. Still, it's not nearly as glamorous as being a high fashion model, and it doesn't pay as well.

Being short isn't a crushing blow or anything. It does mean I have to think about what I want to do once my kid modeling career comes to an end. That was why Kate was talking to me about catalogs.

"That dress will look adorable, Chloe," said Kate. "Go try it on."

I put on the dress and then returned to the studio. Sam had flipped the blue backdrop over to a flowery picture. When I stepped in front of the backdrop, it looked as if I was standing in front of a beautiful garden. Sam took a few quick shots and then we were done. I headed off to the dressing room to change.

I wasn't expected home until six, so I decided to check the Red Room and see if anyone was there. The Red Room is really a photographer's darkroom for developing pictures. It's supposed to be used by Kate Calico's husband. He feels most creative in red light because it reminds him of the old days when photographers had to develop black-and-white pictures in red light. Kate's husband never uses the room, but we do. It's a special hideout where Ashley, Tracey, Nikki, and I go to meet, kill time, do homework, or just hang out.

Stepping into the room, I stumbled over Tracey's long legs. "Step on a person, why don't you?" she scolded, not really mad.

"Sorry," I replied.

Tracey and Nikki were sitting on the floor, looking at a magazine. "My new Cotton Kids ad just came out," Nikki explained, tucking a strand of her long reddish hair behind her ear.

"Let's see," I said, kneeling down beside her. Tracey and Nikki have just begun their modeling careers. They'd both won a model search contest at a mall.

Even though they were new, they were both doing really well. Nikki had been selected as the Cotton Kids spokesteen. She and a boy named Pablo Ruiz were the only two models the Cotton Kids Company used in their ads for junior wear. It was a huge contract.

Tracey was also in demand. While Nikki was the all-American girl, Tracey's look was a little bit tough. But she was pretty, with short, dark brown hair and the most awesome aqua blue eyes. When she was in an ad, you just couldn't take your eyes off it. She has what Kate calls *real presence*. Of all of us, I think the one with the most super-model potential is Tracey. I'd never tell this to Ashley, however. Right now she's the top kid model at the agency, and she's determined to be a super fashion model and maybe even an actress.

"What do you think?" Nikki asked as I looked down at her Cotton Kids ad.

"It's cute," I answered honestly. She was standing on a wooden swing while Pablo pushed her. Her long hair was flying behind her, and her green eyes were sparkling happily. They were both wearing Cotton Kids jogging outfits.

"What are you guys doing here?" I asked.

"We're waiting for Eve," Nikki explained. Eve was Nikki's older stepsister. She usually drove Tracey and Nikki into the city and picked them up after their appointments.

"We got out an hour earlier than we expected, so now we're waiting," Tracey added. "She won't be here until quarter to six."

Just then Ashley came in. "Hi, guys. I'm starved. All I had for lunch was a banana and some granola. I've had back-to-back shoots all day."

"I'm hungry, too," said Tracey. "Want to try that pizzeria around the corner?"

Ashley wrinkled her pretty nose. "That scuzzy place? It looks like a dump."

"Dumps always have the best pizza," said Tracey confidently.

"Is that some sort of rule?" asked Nikki, getting to her feet.

"Yeah," Tracey said with a smile. "It's a Tracey Morris rule. The dumpier the place, the better the pizza."

"I don't know about that," I said. "But pizza sounds good."

We gathered our stuff and headed out of the Red Room. We passed Ms. Calico's big office and the smaller office of Renata Marco, her assistant. We went into the lobby, which was full—as it always seemed to be—of young men and women nervously clutching books of photographs of themselves. They were waiting and hoping for a chance to see Kate and be selected as models.

"Oh, Chloe," the receptionist called to me as I walked past. "There's a message here for you."

I took the pink slip of message paper from her. *Please call Ty Mason,* it read.

"Ty Mason!" I cried excitedly. Ty Mason is the director of "Freshman Bell," a very popular show for teens. A few months back, when Tracey, Nikki, and I visited Ashley in California, I appeared in an episode of the show.

The way I got the part was sort of strange. I was on the beach doing a clothing shoot, and "Freshman Bell" was filming its summer special nearby. After Ashley and I went to watch them, Ty Mason picked me out of the crowd to play a girl who trips over a sand castle. He liked the way I did it, so he added more little parts for me. I became a mystery girl who keeps bumping into things. Soon the character of Scooter, the show's super nerd, falls in love with the mystery girl.

Before I left California, Ty Mason told me he might want to use me in upcoming episodes. But it had been so long since I'd heard from him, I'd forgotten all about it.

"You're going to be on 'Freshman Bell' again!" Ashley cried, clapping her hands.

"How cool," said Tracey as she gave me a thumbs-up.

"Well, I don't know if that's why he's calling," I said, not wanting to get too excited. "Do you really think he wants me? Wouldn't that be great? I don't want to get my hopes up for nothing, but I suppose I have to call him and find out."

"Call him this minute!" said Nikki.

It was no use trying not to be excited. I was *super* excited! "Okay, okay," I agreed nervously. "I'll call him right now."

Chapter Two

———— •◆• ————

As we walked into Arturo's Pizzeria, I saw that Ashley was right. The place was a dump. I didn't care though. How could I care about ripped fabric on the booths or ugly paintings with cracked frames when I was on the verge of stardom?

Okay, well, maybe not *stardom* but something like it. *TV-dom*. And maybe stardom was around the corner.

Tracey stopped by the long steel pizza counter. She pushed back the dark sunglasses she liked to wear so that they rested on top of her head. "Anybody want anything on this pie?"

"Pepperoni," suggested Nikki.

"Yuck," said Ashley.

"Okay, half pepperoni, half plain," Tracey made the compromise. She placed the order, and we scooted into a dingy-looking booth.

"What did he say exactly?" Ashley asked, dusting off the seat we shared. "Tell me every word."

"He said that in the fan mail on the special, a lot of people asked about me and said they'd like to see more of me," I told my friends.

"All right!" Ashley cheered. "Your public is demanding more of you. When the fans want you, you're in."

I smiled. If anyone knew what she was talking about regarding TV, it was Ashley. Her whole family was involved with TV. She had even been in a TV movie.

"I told him I couldn't go to California before school was over, but he said that was no problem. He wants to do an episode where Scooter goes to the city searching for his mystery girl," I continued.

Nikki reached across the table and squeezed my wrist. "This is so unbelievably cool!" she squealed.

"I hope you'll remember us little folks when you're rich and famous," Tracey said.

"I'm the little folk, remember?" I said. "You giants are destined for modeling fame. I'm the one you'll have to remember."

"First, we would never forget you. And second, you don't have to worry anymore," said Ashley confidently. "Maybe you won't be a famous model, but you'll be a famous TV comedian. Maybe you'll get so popular that they'll make a spin-off show about you. I can just see it.

'Chloe's Gang'!"

"Or just 'Chloe,' " Nikki added with a faraway look, as if she was watching the opening credits of the show.

"Hold on, you guys." I laughed. "This is just a guest shot. I'm not even a regular on the show."

"You will be," said Ashley. "It's obvious that they're crazy about you already."

"Would I have to move to California?" I asked anxiously. "I don't think my family would want to do that."

"Don't worry," said Ashley. "Your mother could go out there and get an apartment with you for a while. That would give your dad a chance to sell the restaurant and buy a new one in Hollywood. He's such a great chef, he'd make a fortune out there. Nobody in Hollywood eats at home."

"I don't know about that," I said doubtfully.

"Maybe you'd get so rich from the show that you could fly back and forth," said Nikki.

"Yes! Have that written into your contract," said Ashley. "Sometimes you can do that. The studio has to pay for your trips home."

We continued talking about "Freshman Bell" until our pizza was ready. Tracey was right about the pizza. It was great!

I was on my second slice when a bunch of kids walked into the pizzeria. They were a few years older than us, and they looked pretty tough. One of the guys had a tattoo on his arm. And one of the girls was actually wearing a nose ring. I counted eight of them, and one was meaner looking than the next.

They came and stood in front of our table. "You're sitting in one of our booths," said a tall guy with a red bandanna wrapped around his head, pirate-style. A small gold hoop earring hung from his left ear.

"Listen, Sinbad," said Tracey. "I didn't see any sign on this table saying it was yours."

I nearly croaked! Why did Tracey have to say that?

The guy glared at her menacingly.

"Come on, Slash," called a girl with long jet-black hair who was wearing a leather jacket. "There are plenty of booths."

Slash gave all of us a really mean look, then went to join his friends.

"That was brilliant," I whispered sarcastically to Tracey.

"You can't let guys like that know you're scared of them," Tracey insisted.

"Slash!" gasped Ashley. "Did you hear that? His name is Slash!"

"Shh! Shh!" I hissed at them. "I think they heard you. They're looking over this way." We all stiffened and glanced at them out of the corners of our eyes. Sure enough, the tough kids were talking and staring in our direction.

"They're planning to pulverize us," Ashley whispered anxiously. "Tracey insulted their leader and now we all must die because of it."

"We're not going to die," Tracey snapped back, but there was an edge of nervousness in her voice.

"Don't look at them," Nikki advised. "Let's just eat our pizza and act like we don't care."

We were so stiff that we probably looked like robots as we lifted our slices of pizza and ate. The once-scrumptious pizza now tasted like cardboard to me. I could barely manage to chew it. What a shame to have my budding TV career nipped before it even got started. It's hard to be funny when you're in a body cast.

Every so often, I sneaked a quick glance at their table. They were definitely still talking about us. They were arguing, too. The girl with the long black hair was nodding yes, but Slash kept shaking his head.

I imagined that the girl was telling him to leave us alone, but Slash wasn't about to. "My honor has been challenged," I imagined him saying. "I must get revenge."

Suddenly my heart slammed against my chest. Slash had pushed back his chair and gotten to his feet. "We'll just settle this once and for all," I heard him say.

Ashley grabbed my arm so hard it hurt. "Did you hear what he just said?" she gasped.

"He can't do anything to us in here," said Nikki. "Those pizza guys behind the counter wouldn't let him, would they?"

I glanced at the two guys she was talking about. One was slouched against a table, flipping through a motorcycle magazine. The other had a scar across his cheek and tattoos on both arms. He was talking to someone on the phone. They didn't exactly look like the types to come leaping over the counter to our rescue.

The four of us looked down at our pizza as if it was the most fascinating thing on earth. "When I count to three, get up and run," Ashley said under her breath.

"No way," Tracey argued. "I'm not running from this guy."

"Do you think he could reach us if we hid under the table?" Nikki muttered fearfully.

"I can deal with this guy," said Tracey.

I hoped she was right because he was standing in front of our table. "Hey, girls," said Slash, leaning forward. "We have something to settle. My friends and I want to—"

"We don't care what your friends and you want!" Tracey yelled, jumping to her feet. "Listen here, pal, we have as much right to sit here and not be bothered as you do. So if you don't get that, then get lost!"

To my surprise, Slash stepped back as if Tracey had punched him. It seemed she really *did* know how to handle guys like Slash.

"Well, excuse me," he said, offended. "I didn't mean to bother you. We just wanted to know if that girl there was on 'Freshman Bell.' "

Tracey turned bright pink. "Oh, yeah, that's her," she said in a small voice as she sank down into the booth.

"You're right. It's her!" Slash called back to the kids in his booth.

"Told you so," shouted the girl with the long black hair. At that, the entire table of kids got up and came to our table. The black-haired girl put a napkin and a pen down in front of me. "I thought you were so hysterical," she said. "Could you sign that to Jill, please?"

"Sure," I said, smiling as I began writing.

"She's going to be on the show again," said Nikki, the color slowly coming back to her pale face.

"Really?" Slash said. "When?"

"We're not sure," said Ashley. "Her agent is negotiating with the 'Freshman Bell' people. But we know it will be soon."

A short boy in a leather jacket wanted me to autograph his hand. "When I saw that part where you fell down the stairs, I fell off the couch laughing," he told me. "Where did you learn to fall like that?"

"My brother taught me," I admitted honestly. There had been a lot of falling in my scenes since my character was a total klutz. I'd been able to do it because my brother Matt had taught me to do pratfalls. He'd learned how to do them from a regular restaurant customer of ours who was a stuntman.

By the time I was done, I'd signed autographs for all eight kids. "We'll be watching for you," said Slash as he and his friends went back to their booth.

"Thanks," I said, waving.

"See, they love you out there in TV land," said Ashley.

"I feel like such an idiot," said Tracey.

"No, you were great," I told her. "If we'd needed you to stand up to that guy, you would've been great."

"Yeah, but you didn't," said Tracey. "He wasn't a thug—he was a fan."

"When Chloe is a superstar, you can be her bodyguard." Nikki giggled.

A superstar. I *liked* the sound of that word!

Chapter Three

When I got home that night, I was whisked into another world. You see, my back door leads right into a restaurant kitchen. The restaurant is Chang's Garden, which my family owns. All the family members help out in the restaurant when we're needed. Family life and restaurant life are pretty intermingled.

"Chloe!" my father called in his booming voice as soon as he spotted me. He was in his white chef's outfit. He's such a large man that he reminds me of a giant polar bear when he wears his whites. Sometimes his big voice reminds me of a bear's roar, too. But anyone who *really* knows him isn't fooled. He's more like a teddy bear than anything else.

"What's up, Dad?" I asked.

As he spoke, he never stopped chopping vegetables with his large, sharp cleaver. "Your mother needs help out front."

"Okay," I said, putting down my backpack. I went through the swinging kitchen doors into the restaurant. I was surprised to see that the restaurant was already half full. The dinner crowd usually arrived around seven, and it was only just after six. What were all these people doing here so early?

My mother was busy taking money at the register while Sue, the waitress, waited on the tables. The second waitress, Agnes, wouldn't come in until seven. "Hi, sweetheart," said Mom. "Could you clear tables and pick up checks for Sue? Just until Agnes gets here."

"Sure," I said. "Why is it so busy?"

"Spring, I guess," she said. "You know, the tourists start coming down to walk around when the weather gets nice. And then there was that write-up in the paper." Our restaurant had been featured in a column called "Best Restaurants" that ran in the Saturday edition of the *City Sun* newspaper.

I spent the next half hour clearing dirty dishes from tables and putting them into a big plastic tub. From time to time, my brother Matt would come out of the kitchen and grab a tub and take it back in. Then he'd stack the dishes in the dishwasher and bring out a rack of clean dishes.

That's what I meant about being in a different world. It's a little weird to go from being a model and signing autographs to wrapping yourself in a white apron and clearing away dirty dishes, getting water for people, and delivering change.

I didn't mind doing it, though. I've helped out at the restaurant since I was six. Everyone in my family did. For a while, when I was little, I thought everyone worked with their parents. I like it this way. My parents are always around, even if they are incredibly busy most of the time.

"Hello, Flower," said my grandma as I was stacking some plates in a tub. Flower is her pet name for me.

"Hi, Grandma," I said with a smile. My grandma is one of my favorite people. She's a tiny lady with the spirit of a lioness. When her dark eyes look at you from her wrinkled face, you feel like she can see right into you. And those eyes are always full of life and laughter.

Grandma relieved Mom at the register, and Mom started helping Sue with customers. The people kept coming and coming. It was an incredibly busy night.

I noticed one woman in her early twenties who kept staring at me. "Can I get you something?" I asked her. "Do you need water?"

"Were you on 'Freshman Bell'?" the woman asked.

"Yes," I admitted with a small smile.

"And they're going to do more episodes, right?" said the woman, pushing aside a strand of her blunt-cut coppery hair.

"How did you know that?" I asked.

"Their press people called me this afternoon."

"What?" I asked, not understanding.

The woman smiled and extended her hand. "I'm Lisa Waters. I'm a writer with the *City Sun*. I do their entertainment column. Would you be interested in an interview?"

"Me?" I asked, flattered.

"Sure. You're a model, too, aren't you?"

"Yes. How did you know *that?*"

"The press people told me, but they didn't tell me you work in a restaurant at night. That's a really interesting angle for the story."

"I don't always," I explained. "This is my family's place, and I help out when I'm needed."

"It would be great publicity for the restaurant," she said. "Although it looks as if you have all the customers you can handle. Still, a story like this could really make the place famous. It will bring in movie and TV people."

I thought of what Ashley had said about Dad moving the restaurant to Los Angeles. Maybe if he became a super success here, and all his customers were famous, that move would be easier. Then I would be free to go out there and be a regular on "Freshman Bell."

"Sure," I said. "When?"

Lisa Waters thought a moment. "I'll have to squeeze this in Wednesday evening. Would you be free around seven?"

"I guess so," I said. "I'm going to see the 'Freshman

Bell' people Monday afternoon, so I'll know more about things."

"Super," said Lisa. "I'll be here with a photographer. Is that okay?"

"Yeah," I said. At that moment, I noticed Mom looking at me sternly. I realized I'd been gabbing while dirty dishes were piling up on tables. A line of waiting customers had formed at the front door. "Got to go," I told Lisa. "See you Wednesday."

The dinner customers just kept pouring in. Even when Agnes arrived, we were busy. "Do you have schoolwork?" Mom asked me around eight-thirty. I nodded. "Then go do it."

"Don't you need help?" I asked.

"We'll manage," said Mom. "Schoolwork is important. Scoot!"

I took off my apron as I went through the kitchen. Matt was still busy stacking the dishwasher. My younger brother, Tommy, was helping him. My other brother, Henry, was working with Dad. Dad's training him to be a chef, too. "Did your mother say you could leave?" Dad asked, never looking up from the slivered pork he was cooking.

"Yeah. I have homework," I told him.

"All right, then. Send Michelle down. She's upstairs baby-sitting Amanda."

I climbed the narrow stairs and went to our second-floor apartment. Michelle was lying on the living room couch with an incredibly thick textbook on her lap. She's in her first year of medical school and seems to be studying every second. "Dad wants you to help out downstairs," I told her.

Michelle sighed and flipped her long French braid back behind her shoulder. "I suppose I need a break from this anyway," she said, rubbing her eyes. "Mandy is asleep."

"Good," I said. "Because I have a ton of homework."

I checked on my younger sister, then went to my room and did my math homework. I also read the chapter I'd been assigned in social studies. Finally I opened my English textbook and reread the assignment: Write an essay about the person in your life you most admire. It wasn't due until Wednesday, but it would be best to get it out of the way. With "Freshman Bell" and my interview coming up, I figured I'd be pretty busy between now and then.

Lying back on my bed, I wondered who I admired most. I admired Johnny Renee, Ashley's TV-star brother. However, I didn't think Mrs. Elmont, my teacher, had meant *admire* in that sense. What I admired about him were his muscles and handsome face. I could have written a ten-page essay about how gorgeous he is, but I knew Mrs. Elmont wouldn't appreciate it.

Kate Calico came to mind. She was so sophisticated

and stylish. She was also a successful businesswoman. I could write my essay about her.

Then I thought of Grandma. I admired how she was always helping people in the neighborhood, bringing them her special herb teas when they were sick. People said they really worked.

When Grandma was younger, she'd studied medicine in China. She never got to be a doctor, but she knew a lot. She even knew about delivering babies. She'd helped my mother when I'd been born right in this very apartment.

Yes, Grandma would be a good person to write about. I realized, though, that I really didn't know all that much about her. Isn't it odd that you can live so close to someone and not know everything about her? If I wanted to write about her, I'd have to interview her.

Just then I heard the front door open and shut. I got off the bed, hoping it was Grandma. Even though she and Grandpa live above us, they often come to our apartment.

I ran to the living room, but it was Michelle and Tommy. "Things finally died down," said Michelle, yawning.

"Is Grandma still down there?" I asked.

"No, she went up to her place," Tommy told me.

I hurried upstairs and knocked on Grandma's door. "It's Chloe," I called.

Grandma opened the door. I could see she'd been getting ready for bed. She'd already changed into a flowery robe. Her long white hair was loose and fell around her shoulders. "Come in, Flower," she said.

I stepped into the dark, cozy apartment. Even though it was as big as our apartment, it seemed much smaller. That was probably because Grandma and Grandpa had stuffed it with the things they'd collected over the years. A plush red, blue, and green rug with a swirling dragon at its center hung on one wall. The furniture was made of a thick, dark reddish wood. The shelves, made of the same wood, were crowded with ivory carvings, jeweled boxes, and delicate statues.

The apartment smelled of the herbs Grandma was always brewing or grinding into a powder. Sometimes it smelled heavenly, like lavender, or sweet like chamomile. Other times it had the deep, pungent smell of ginseng.

"Do you want a cup of tea?" Grandma asked, moving into her kitchen. She turned on her tape player, and soft Chinese music filled the apartment.

"No, thanks," I said. "In school, we have to write an essay on a person who . . . um . . ." I was surprised to find that I was embarrassed to tell her I admired her. "A person in our family. So I picked you."

"Oh, I'm flattered," she said, perching on a stool. At that moment, the phone rang. "Excuse me," said Grandma, picking up her kitchen wall phone. In seconds, she was speaking rapid-fire Chinese, which I'd never learned more than a few words of. "That was Mr. Fong," she explained after she hung up. "Mrs. Fong has had a respiratory problem for two weeks now. She's been to the doctor, but the medicine isn't working."

"What will you give her?" I asked.

"I'll have to see her first before I can figure out what would be best," Grandma replied. "Now, was there something you wanted to ask me?"

"I need to know some things about—"

I was interrupted by the sound of Grandpa calling from the bedroom. He's ten years older than Grandma and pretty sickly. "Just a moment," Grandma said to me. "His humidifier probably ran dry."

She hurried off to attend to Grandpa. I sat looking around her kitchen. A beautiful calendar was tacked to the wall. On it was a painting of a pagoda with trees blossoming all around. Grandma's favorite teapot sat near the stove. I could see why she liked it. It was in the shape of a dragon and covered with a deep red enamel glaze. When the tea was ready, it looked like steam was coming out of the dragon's nose.

It was funny how although she lived right above us, I felt as if I were stepping into another time and place when I stepped into her apartment.

I waited and waited. Finally I became worried. Was Grandpa all right? I went into the living room and found

Grandma sitting on the couch, fast asleep. "Grandma," I said, shaking her gently. She sputtered and stirred but didn't wake up.

I checked on Grandpa asleep in their bed. His humidifier whirred quietly by the bedside. He snored softly. I shut the door and went back to Grandma. As gently as I could, I put her feet up on the couch and put the throw blanket over her. Then I snapped off the light and went back downstairs. My essay would have to wait until tomorrow.

Chapter Four

———◆———

his is too cool! Too cool!"
said Ashley on Monday afternoon. We were going up the
elevator to the KVG studios. "Did you see that guy getting
off the elevator? I think he's the guy who plays Skylar
Martin on 'The Beautiful and Wild.' "

By the time we got to studio C, Ashley had spotted two
other people from TV, although I didn't recognize either of
them. Inside the studio doors, Michelle was waiting for me.
My mother was busy, but she didn't want me going there
alone. "Hi, Michelle," I greeted her.

"Hi," she said. "Listen, do you mind if I sit by this
entrance and study? If you need me for anything, I'll be
right here reading, okay?"

"We won't need you," Ashley assured her. "These people adore Chloe. They'll do whatever she says."

Just then the director, Ty Mason, spotted us. "Chloe, kiddo, how are you?" he called as he approached us. "Glad to see you."

"Hi. Do you remember my friend, Ashley Taylor?" I asked.

"Sure, nice to see you again," he said to Ashley. I liked Mr. Mason. He'd been really nice to me the last time I was on the show. "I'm so glad you can do this," he said. "The mail has just been pouring in after the summer special. They love you out there in TV land."

"That's great," I said with a smile.

Ashley and I followed him deeper into the studio. We went through another set of doors and into a room with black walls. By the far wall was a set with bright lights trained on it. The set looked like a city street. It was unbelievably realistic. "There it is," Mr. Mason said proudly. "Your home in Chinatown!"

A second look showed me that all the signs on the set stores were in Chinese. "It's nice," I said. "But why not film in the real Chinatown, since you're here?"

"We will be filming some scenes on location, but it's easier to film on a set," Mr. Mason explained. "We don't have to worry about cars and crowds. Besides, I looked at Chinatown, and it lacks a certain Chinese-ness. I'm looking for more pagodas, dragons, paper umbrellas—

that sort of thing."

"We have those," I said.

"Yes, but not enough of them. I want this set to be an explosion of Chinese stuff. Viewers have to know right away where they are."

That made sense, I supposed. At that moment, two crew members came onto the set and strung an immense paper dragon between two of the set buildings. Then two men came and put a big sign in a store window. It showed a picture of a man with long fingernails and a long, thin mustache. "In the story, Scooter wants to make you fall in love with him, so he goes to an herbalist to get a love potion tea," said Mr. Mason.

He smiled as if he expected me to crack up at that idea, but I didn't. It didn't make sense to me. "Herbalists don't make love potions," I said.

"Kiddo, this is a comedy," said Mr. Mason. "Reality isn't important. What matters is that it's funny."

"I guess," I agreed, wanting to be cooperative.

Mr. Mason called to his assistant. "Terry, give Chloe her script." A thin young woman hurried over and handed me a thick script. "Don't worry," Mr. Mason told me. "You appear a lot, but you don't say much. Remember, you're still the mystery girl of Scooter's dreams."

I opened the script and looked through it. I didn't even have a name. My part was just called Mystery Girl. I didn't appear at all in the first act, which was all about

Scooter and his friends trying to locate me. It wasn't until the second act that I finally spoke. My first line was "Ah so." "Ah so?" I questioned Mr. Mason.

"Don't Chinese people say that?" Mr. Mason replied.

"I've never heard anyone say it," I explained.

Mr. Mason opened his script to the spot and circled the line. "I'll mention that to the scriptwriters."

"And this line about my brother being a judo master isn't really right," I pointed out. "Judo is a Japanese form of martial arts. Kung fu is the Chinese form."

"I'll make a note of that," Mr. Mason explained.

I looked further on in the script. My character worked in her family's laundry. "I don't think this scene is exactly right," I said. In the scene, Scooter leaves his T-shirt in the family's laundry. He comes back to get it, and she won't let him have it without the ticket. "The few Chinese laundries left in my neighborhood are computerized. They'd cross-reference his order by name and then ask for identification," I said.

Mr. Mason frowned. "That's not exactly funny, though, is it?"

"I suppose not, but still . . ." I said.

He marked the spot in his script. "I know—she can unveil this super state-of-the-art computer system. Everyone knows Asians love electronic gizmos. This computer can be so sophisticated that it takes his picture, spot cleans the shirt he's wearing, and prints out his name, address, and phone number. Something really wild would be even funnier. Thanks, Chloe, you just gave me a great idea."

"You're welcome," I said. But I wasn't sure I was in love with this idea. Between the ah so, the love potion, the judo, the laundry, and the ridiculous computer, I could see that the writers were treating being Chinese as if it was some sort of joke.

Someone called Ty Mason away for a moment. "Don't worry," said Ashley. " 'Freshman Bell' is a big hit. These guys know what they're doing. Once Ty Mason talks to the writers, I'm sure they'll take out the offensive stuff. Remember when we were in California and my dad was shooting that movie?"

"Yes," I said, nodding.

"Well, he was ordering script changes every few days. It's part of the process."

"I hope you're right," I said.

"Sure I'm right," Ashley assured me.

"I don't want to embarrass myself or my family," I said, feeling worried.

"No way," said Ashley. "These guys are pros."

As we spoke, a very thin woman with frizzy brown curls came hurrying into the studio. "Ty!" she called. "Ty, I must speak to you."

"That's Koozy Curtis," Ashley told me, obviously impressed.

"Koozy whoosy?" I asked.

"Curtis! She's the host of 'Kids Talk!' It's a new interview and dance show for kids our age. Where have you been?"

"I don't know," I said with a shrug. "It must be on when someone else in my family's favorite show is on. I never saw it."

"Well, it's big," Ashley said confidently. "My mother just interviewed her on *her* show."

"What is it, Koozy?" Mr. Mason asked, rushing over to Koozy Curtis.

"Ty, my big guest can't make it. Her flight was canceled. You've got to lend me one of your kids. I have five minutes to fill and no star."

"Interview Chloe," Mr. Mason suggested, pointing to me.

Koozy Curtis looked at me and wrinkled her face in dismay. "Who is she?" she asked.

"She's our newest star," said Mr. Mason. "She was on the summer special and she was a smash. We want to promote her because we'll be using her quite often in the future. She might even become a regular."

"I don't know," said Koozy, looking at me doubtfully.

"Trust him," Ashley said firmly. "She's going to be huge."

"The kid's right about that," said Mr. Mason. "A month from now, you won't be able to get an interview with her.

Believe me, you want to beat everyone else by getting her on your show first."

His words convinced Ms. Curtis, and her frosty face melted into a smile. "Chloe, dear, come with me," she said. "You're about to be the featured guest on 'Kids Talk!' "

Ashley patted my shoulder. "Way to go, future star!"

Chapter Five

---◆---

Talk about fast! From the second Koozy Curtis put her hand on my arm, I was in a whirlwind. She hurried me out of the "Freshman Bell" studio and down the hall to the studio where they taped "Kids Talk!" Ashley followed us, but Koozy hardly noticed her.

In about three minutes, the makeup person put mascara on my lashes, pink lipstick on my lips, and blusher on my cheeks. The hairstylist squirted white hills of mousse all over my head and then spiked my short black hair into peaks. "This isn't really me," I objected.

"You look totally cool," said Ashley, who stood next to me.

"Are you sure?" I asked.

"Completely," said Ashley.

The wardrobe woman decided that my black-and-white capri-length stretch pants were fine, but she wanted me to change from my black turtleneck into a red tunic. Two young women came in and helped get the top over my head without messing my hair and makeup. I felt like a princess with servants dressing me.

Just as my head came through the top of the tunic, Koozy Curtis rushed into the room. "You look adorable," she said as she guided me out of the chair. "Let's go, let's go! There's only three minutes to airtime. You have to be in your seat and ready for the interview."

Koozy began to run. Ashley and I ran after her. "What are you going to ask me?" I asked Koozy.

"I don't quite know yet," she admitted. "I'll think of something."

When we got to the main part of the studio, I saw a blinking red sign. It read: ON AIR. "Go! Go!" the show's producer whispered urgently to us. Ashley joined the crowd of kids sitting on bleachers around the stage. I ran up onto a one-foot-high platform and sat in one of the two chairs set up on the stage.

"Hi! Koozy Curtis here!" Koozy spoke to the camera. "Get ready for 'Kids Talk!'" Another sign overhead blinked the message: APPLAUSE-CHEERS. The TV audience couldn't see it, but the studio audience could. The kids started clapping and cheering. When the sign went off, they stopped.

"My guest today is supermodel and comedy star Chloe Chang," Koozy said. Supermodel? Comedy star? Not quite. But I guess Koozy had to make me sound important or no one would want to hear about me. "You've seen Chloe on countless magazine covers," she continued. "And you've seen her on the 'Freshman Bell' summer special. Well, you'll be seeing a lot more of Chloe, because she's a star who's going places!"

Koozy took her seat onstage next to me. "So, Chloe," she said with a warm smile, "I'm sure all the girls in our audience are interested in the beauty secrets of a supermodel. What are your special beauty routines?"

"Well, I'm not exactly a supermodel," I objected.

Koozy tapped my knee and laughed lightly. "Of course, you are. Don't be modest. Just give us a few beauty tips."

She couldn't have asked me a worse question. I didn't have any tips. "I don't know," I said. "Nothing really."

It was just a flicker, but I saw anger fire up in Koozy's eyes.

"Well," I said, searching my mind desperately for a tip. "I wash my face every night." Then I noticed Ashley hopping up and down in the front row. I squinted through the bright lights to see her better. She was bending forward and throwing her hair over her face.

At first I thought she'd lost her mind. Then I realized what she was trying to tell me. "Oh, and when I blow-dry my hair, I bend over and blow it forward. That makes it seem much fuller when I brush it back."

Koozy faced the camera. "Got that, girls?" She turned back toward me. "Any other tips?"

I looked back to Ashley for help. With big gestures, she was pretending to put on lipstick, and then she was dotting her cheeks. I didn't get it. "I . . . uh . . . wear light-colored lipstick when I'm working, but not in my regular life," I said, sensing that Koozy was impatiently waiting for me to say something . . . anything!

I suddenly realized what Ashley was telling me. "Oh, and if you don't have a blusher that matches your shade of lipstick, you can put a few dots of your lipstick on your cheekbones. It works almost as well as a blusher if you blend it in." I'd never done this, but I knew Ashley did it all the time.

"Excellent!" Koozy exclaimed. "I'll try that one myself."

Luckily she got off beauty tips and went on to ask me about my role on "Freshman Bell." "My character is sort of a klutz, but she's very sweet," I explained. "In the special, Scooter fell in love with her. Now he's come to the city to find her. That's all I really know, because I haven't read the script yet."

"We'll all look forward to seeing you," said Koozy. "We know there are big things in your future." She faced the camera. "Kids, you saw her interviewed here first! Remember, keep your eye on Chloe Chang as she rockets to superstardom!"

She turned back to me, and I realized I was supposed to say something. "Thanks, everybody," I said with a smile and a wave.

A blast of rock music filled the room. "Chloe, why don't you join the kids for our dance moment," Koozy said for all to hear.

"Sure," I replied, getting into the mood. They were playing a brand-new song by my favorite group.

Feeling happy that the interview was over, I danced down off the stage into the crowd. I was planning to dance with Ashley, but she'd already found a cute boy in the crowd. A tall boy with light brown hair made his way over to me, and I started dancing with him.

He was cute and a good dancer. I really broke loose and matched his energetic steps. When he began playing air guitar, I went along with him and lip-synched the words to the song as I danced. I pretended I was belting out every word like a real rock star.

I was giving it all I had when something made me stop. I had noticed Ashley staring at me with a serious face. What was wrong? I wondered. She was jerking her thumb off to the right. I looked in that direction and nearly fainted.

Ashley had been pointing at the TV monitor mounted near the ceiling. It showed the actual picture that was on TV. And what the camera was showing was *me*. Just me, alone! I'd thought I would be lost in the crowd of dancing kids. But they were showing me goofing around, lip-synching.

The camera stayed right on me. I couldn't think of anything else to do, so I kept on singing and dancing. I mean, I couldn't just stand there like a dummy with the camera on me like that. Only now I wasn't nearly as wild. I just sort of shuffled back and forth pretending to sing.

After what seemed like a zillion years, the song ended.

"We'll be back after this word from our sponsors," Koozy said to the camera. "Don't go away."

The blinking sign that had said ON AIR now blinked another message: BREAK. Koozy hurried over to me. "Chloe, you were marvelous," she gushed.

"I'm sorry about the singing," I apologized. "I didn't know the camera would be on me. I hope I didn't look too stupid."

"That's all right. You looked adorable. It was great. Do you really sing?"

"Like a toad," I admitted. "Everyone knew I was just fooling around, didn't they?"

"Sure they did," said Koozy. Just then I noticed Michelle come into the studio.

"Would you like to stay for the rest of the show?" Koozy invited me and Ashley.

"No, I'd better get going," I said. "I didn't expect to be here at all. And I should talk to Mr. Mason before I go."

"Well, it was a pleasure meeting you," said Koozy. "You, too, Amy."

"Ashley," Ashley corrected her with a slight snarl.

"Thanks for your help," I told Ashley as we walked over to where Michelle was waiting by the door. "I would have sat there like an idiot if you hadn't given me those beauty tips."

Ashley put her arm around me. "No problem. You did great. That lip-synching business was a riot, too."

"I didn't look like a jerk?"

"Not at all," said Ashley. "Don't worry. Everyone will know you were just kidding. It's not a big deal."

"I hope so," I said.

When I reached Michelle, I saw that she had brought my thick script with her. "Mr. Mason said to memorize your lines, and he'll see you on Thursday at four o'clock," she said, handing me the script.

"How did he know you were my sister?" I asked.

Michelle shrugged. "I don't know. Maybe because I was the only other Chinese person there."

"Ah so," I said knowingly, testing how it felt to say that.

Michelle gave me a strange look.

"That's one of my lines," I explained.

"You're actually going to say that?" Michelle asked in disbelief.

"Well, Mr. Mason said the writers might change it," I told her.

49

"I should certainly hope so," said Michelle as we walked out of the studio.

"You don't have to get all huffy about it," I said. Even though I thought the line was a stupid stereotype of Chinese people, I didn't like Michelle saying anything about it. I didn't want her criticizing "Freshman Bell"— the show that was about to rocket me to superstardom!

Chapter Six

Yes, Mrs. Elmont. I know it's late. I'm sorry," I said. It was Wednesday morning and my English class had just ended. Mrs. Elmont had asked me to stay after class. She wanted to know why I didn't have my essay on the person I admired most.

"You know, Chloe, at the last parent-teacher conference, your parents told me they were very concerned about your modeling interfering with your schoolwork. Is that the problem?" Mrs. Elmont asked, looking at me sternly from behind her thick glasses.

"No, no," I assured her anxiously. "Well, sort of, but only partly. I've been busy, but so has my grandmother. She's even busier than I am. I haven't been able to find a moment to talk to her about her life, and I need to do that before I can write my essay."

"But you knew the essay was due today," Mrs. Elmont insisted.

"Yes, but I forgot," I admitted.

"You forgot?"

"You see, I'm going to be on TV again, which is very important to me since I'm afraid my modeling career might be running out because of my size and all." It was no use. I could see from her icy expression that Mrs. Elmont didn't understand. "I've had a lot on my mind," I ended dismally.

"This is just the kind of thing your parents are worried about," said Mrs. Elmont. "I think I should call them and discuss ways in which your schedule can be cut back to—"

"No!" I jumped in frantically. "Please don't do that. Last marking period I got a C in history, and my father almost drove me crazy. Please don't call them. If I could just have more time, I promise to get the essay in."

"That's not exactly fair to the other students who handed it in on time," said Mrs. Elmont.

"What if I start with a B?" I suggested. "That would even things up."

"I suppose so," Mrs. Elmont agreed. "All right. You have until Friday. Don't forget."

"I won't," I told her happily. "Thank you. I won't forget again."

For a moment, as I walked out the door, I was happy. My parents wouldn't have to know about this. Then reality hit me. I was starting with a B. In order to keep the B, the essay would have to be perfect. If my grade dropped to a C, my father would start hounding me to do my work and threaten to bring my modeling career to an early close. I'm sure he'd say the same thing about my TV career, as well. Schoolwork was extremely important to him.

When I got home that afternoon, the first words out of my mouth were, "Where's Grandma?"

"She took Amanda out for a walk," said my mother, who was sitting at the kitchen counter breaking open fresh pea pods and pouring the small green peas into a big steel colander.

I sighed deeply and threw up my arms in frustration.

"What's wrong?" Mom asked.

"I need to write an essay about her life, and it's due in two days," I said, deciding it was best not to mention that it was *already* late. "Could you tell me some things about Grandma?"

Mom kept snapping open pods. "What kinds of things?"

"You know, about her life," I said as I pulled over a stool and began snapping the peas along with her.

Mom gazed at the ceiling as if she was trying to recall. "Well, she was born in 1920 in one of the northern provinces of China, just outside a city that is now called Shenyang."

This didn't mean an awful lot to me. I would have to look at a map. But 1920 sure seemed like a long time ago. It was hard to believe that my grandmother had actually been alive then. "Things must have been very different then," I commented.

Mom smiled. "Very different. Grandma's family was quite well educated and old-fashioned. They had more money than most. In fact, by the standards of the times and the area, they were wealthy."

"Then why aren't Grandma and Grandpa really wealthy now?" I asked.

"A lot of things happened," said Mom. "The Communist revolution changed things in China. The upper classes were attacked as being the enemies of the common people. Anyone who was seen as an intellectual was persecuted. The Communist revolutionaries saw anyone who wasn't a farmer or a laborer as suspect."

"What happened to Grandma's family?" I asked.

"Grandma's father, my grandfather, was a smart man. By late in 1948, he knew his family was headed for trouble. Most of his property had already been taken from him. He still had an art import and export business in Hong Kong, though. So he told the local Communist party leader that he had to go to Hong Kong to sell the business. He promised to come back and hand over the money. I guess the party leader believed him because he was leaving behind his house and all his possessions. He took the whole family with him, and they didn't return."

"Wow!" I gasped. "They left *everything* behind?"

Mom nodded. "Things can be replaced. Lives can't. My

grandfather had heard of other members of the upper classes who had been shot."

"But why was it safe in Hong Kong?" I asked.

"Because Hong Kong was held by the British," Mom explained.

"Is that where Grandma learned about medicine?"

Mom shook her head sadly. "No, that's where she stopped learning about medicine. There was barely enough money left in the business to get them out of China. There was certainly no money left for medical school."

"So she studied in America?" I questioned.

"No, Grandma studied in China before the revolution. She battled her family hard for that right, too. Back then, China was even more backward than the U.S. was in terms of women's equality. A rich Chinese girl was expected to get married, nothing more. And that was all. But Grandma was stubborn. She refused to marry anyone."

Mom stopped talking and laughed. "If it looked like her parents were going to insist, she would make herself so disagreeable that the future groom would back away. Besides that, she was always sneaking off to talk to the local herbalists and midwives, who taught her a lot. Her family didn't know how to deal with her. Finally, when she was past twenty-four and still not married, her parents gave in. They let her go to a medical school and study. But she never became a doctor. The Communist revolution interrupted all that."

"Why didn't she continue studying in America?" I asked.

"She couldn't speak the language at first. Her family arrived with almost no money. She had to help support her younger brothers and sisters. The only job she could find was working as a laundress in a Chinese laundry."

"How terrible," I said. "Didn't things get better after a while?"

"Yes, but by then I was born, and then my two sisters. Instead of spending what money she and Grandpa had on her own education, she started putting it away for us."

"What a life!" I said. No wonder Grandma had so many wrinkles.

At that moment, Grandma came in through the front restaurant door, holding a brown paper bag. Amanda toddled along beside her.

"Grandma, hi!" I said. "Do you have a minute?"

"Not really," Grandma said as she unpacked her bag. She laid the plastic bags of herbs on the table. "Mrs. Fong's respiratory problem is getting worse. But I think I know what will help her." She went to the kitchen sink and filled a kettle with water, then set it on the stove to boil.

"I want to ask you some things about your life," I said.

"Oh, yes, your essay. Well, that's important. I'm sorry I fell asleep the other night before we could talk," Grandma said. "What do you want to know?"

I grabbed a pen and notebook from my backpack. "When did you first decide to study medicine?"

"The day I was born," she replied, chopping the buds off the long, stringy chamomile and putting them in the food processor.

"No, seriously," I said.

"I am serious," she insisted as the processor whirred. "As long as I can remember, I tended animals, even insects with broken wings. One day my father took me on a trip, and our carriage broke down in a poor village. While it was being fixed, I watched an old woman heal a wheezing child by placing four sharp needles in different spots on his foot. Within a half hour, the boy started breathing normally. I decided then and there that I would become a doctor and take care of people who were too poor to afford doctors. But it never happened."

"How come you didn't—" I began, but I was interrupted by the phone. Grandma answered it and began talking in Chinese.

"I'm sorry, Flower," she said after she hung up. "Mr. Fong is really worried about his wife. He took her to the emergency room, but it was so crowded he brought her home again. I have to get over there."

Just then the crash of pots made me turn. Amanda had gotten into the storage closet again. She loved opening drawers and closets and pulling out everything inside. "Chloe, would you take Amanda upstairs and watch her until I get up there?" said Mom, lifting Amanda out of the pots.

"When do you think you'll be back?" I asked Grandma.

"I don't know," said Grandma. "By seven, I suppose."

"All right, I'll talk to you then," I said. But as I took Amanda to our apartment, I remembered that Lisa Waters and her photographer were coming at seven to interview me. How would I get ready and watch Amanda at the same time? "Come on, Amanda," I said. "I've got to get dressed."

"I no pest!" she shouted.

"Not *pest!* Dressed!" I tried to explain, but Amanda kept frowning at me. "Oh, never mind," I said, scooping her into my arms. "Let's just go."

I ran up the stairs. I would never be ready in time!

Chapter Seven

———◆———

You were fabulous on 'Kids Talk!' " said Lisa Waters. "You have real stage presence, you know."

"Thanks," I said. We were sitting in my living room for the interview. On the coffee table in front of the couch, Lisa had placed a tiny silver tape recorder. Its small tape turned silently, recording our every word. Almost as silent was the photographer, who moved around the couch taking pictures of me from every angle.

"Let's talk about modeling," said Lisa. "Do you miss having a normal kid's life?"

"No," I said. "My life *is* normal. It's just busy."

"But what about friends? Do you have time for any?"

"Oh, sure I do," I told her. "I'm friendly with some kids at school, but my really close friends are other models. We do lots of stuff together. My friend Ashley came with me to the taping of 'Kids Talk!' "

"You don't mean Ashley Taylor, the daughter of Taylor Andrews, do you?" Lisa asked.

"Yes, she's my best friend."

"Yet your lives must be very different," Lisa pointed out astutely.

"Yes, they are," I agreed. "Ashley is a very busy model. Everyone wants to work with her because she's so pretty and professional. Modeling is her whole life. It's all she really thinks about. I'm not like that, though. She's much more devoted to her career than I am."

"You're more well-rounded," Lisa suggested.

"I wouldn't say that," I disagreed. "But I go to regular school, unlike Ashley, who has a tutor. And I have my work here at the restaurant. Besides, I'm not sure I'll continue modeling as an adult. I might do something else."

"Like be a major TV star?" said Lisa.

"That would be nice," I said with a smile. "But if that doesn't happen, I'll do something else. Lots of kid models have other plans. My good friend Tracey Morris is extremely smart, and there are lots of other fields she might go into. Sometimes I can hardly believe she's a model. She's interested in so many other things besides fashion or makeup or hair. Yet she's very pretty and a great model."

"But you do like modeling, don't you?" Lisa asked.

"Oh, yes, I love it. It's opened so many opportunities for

me. A lot of the kids feel that way. Take my friend Nikki Wilton, for example. She's completely amazed by everything that's happened to her since she became a model. Before that, she'd never traveled anywhere, never even been on a plane. She'd never really done anything compared to the kinds of things she's seen and experienced as a successful model."

"What's it like to work for Kate Calico?" Lisa asked.

"The best," I told her. "At first, people think she's a real slave driver, but that's just because she wants Calico models to be tops. After you get to know her, you find out she's very kindhearted."

"All right, tell me all about your upcoming role on 'Freshman Bell,' " said Lisa.

I told her what little I knew. Talking about the show reminded me that I hadn't begun to memorize my lines. And the first rehearsal was tomorrow! I'd have to spend all of tonight memorizing them. Well, I already knew one. Ah so! But that line would probably be gone by the time the rehearsals began.

At that moment, my mother came up the stairs holding Amanda, who was sound asleep, her head slumped on Mom's shoulder. Mom had met Lisa earlier down in the restaurant. "How's the interview going?" she asked.

Lisa snapped off her tape recorder. "I think we're done. I have enough information to write a nice article. Do you have all the pictures you need, Len?"

The photographer nodded. "All set."

"Would you like a soda, or tea or coffee?" Mom asked.

"No thanks," said Lisa. "I'd better go back home and write this article up. It will be in tomorrow's paper."

"Tomorrow!" I gasped, surprised it would appear so soon.

"Yep. I told them to keep two columns open for me. I'll just use my computer modem to zap it into the computers down at work. It will be typeset and ready by press time tonight and printed and on the stands by tomorrow morning."

"Modern technology is amazing," Mom commented.

"It certainly is," said Lisa. "Thanks for your time."

When she was gone, Mom put Amanda to bed. Then she came back into the living room. "Lisa was really nice," I said to Mom as she began sorting through the mail she'd brought up with her.

"I suppose," said Mom.

"You didn't think so?"

"I don't always trust people who don't make eye contact with you," Mom said quietly. I tried to remember if Lisa had looked me in the eye. I wasn't sure if she had or not. I'd been too busy thinking about what I was going to say next.

"Well, I thought she was nice," I insisted.

"You're probably right," said Mom. "By the way, Chloe, if you want to talk to Grandma now, she went up to her apartment."

"I can't tonight," I said. "I've got to memorize my 'Freshman Bell' lines."

"Do you have any homework to do?" Mom asked.

"No," I said, which was true. I'd done it all in study hall that afternoon. My only homework was the essay, but that wasn't due until Friday. I still had another day.

I went to my room and found the script sitting on my dresser. I began by going through it with a yellow highlighter and marking all the lines for Mystery Girl. Some of them were pretty dumb. The dumbest was when my character wants to order Chinese noodles in a pizzeria. What kind of idiot would do that? I didn't like it. I decided to ask Mr. Mason to have it changed. He seemed willing to listen to what I had to say.

It took me two hours to get my lines down. It seemed sort of a waste of time since so many of them would change by the time the show was really taped. But I guessed Mr. Mason had his reasons for wanting me to memorize the script the way it was.

I wanted to ask someone to read through the script with me, but the lines were so dopey, I was embarrassed. My family wouldn't understand that the really stupid lines were going to change.

Closing the script, I sat back on my bed. So much was happening. Down on the floor was a celebrity magazine that I liked to browse through. Would I ever be on the cover? I didn't mean as a model, but as a celebrity.

Celebrities were always going to fancy parties with other celebrities. They were rich and beautiful, and everyone loved them.

They weren't tucked away in petite clothing catalogs.

They didn't work in restaurants clearing dirty dishes off tables.

Suddenly the possibility of doing either of those things as a career sounded horrible. But if I didn't become a celebrity, there was a good chance that one of them was exactly what I would wind up doing.

I was so close to being a celebrity, too. I could see it so clearly. I'd have a huge white house filled with servants. I'd have a pool bigger than the one Ashley's dad had out in California. Her brother, Johnny Renee, would look at me differently, too. I wouldn't be just a little kid—I'd be another star, and his equal. Maybe I'd be an even bigger star than he was.

I wouldn't change, of course. I'd still be me. I'd invite Ashley, Tracey, and Nikki to come live with me. It would be like a never-ending slumber party. All of us would enjoy my celebrity status together.

Leaning back against my headboard, I closed my eyes and hugged my script. I was almost there. If I did well on "Freshman Bell," I'd be a star for sure.

Chapter Eight

Ashley, what's the matter?"
I asked as I hurried down the hall of the Calico agency
behind her. Her legs are longer than mine, and she was
moving quickly. It was hard to keep up with her.

She kept walking and didn't even turn around. I stopped
alongside her and then in front, blocking her. "I'm not
talking to you," she said coolly, dodging out of my path.

"Why not?" I exploded. "What did I do?"

"Like you don't know."

"What?" I asked. "Tell me. You were talking to me
yesterday, and nothing has happened since then."

"Oh, no?" she said icily.

With her perfect model's nose in the air, she headed
toward the Red Room. I was right behind her and slipped
into the room with her.

Nikki and Tracey were already there. They looked at me and their eyes narrowed angrily. I felt as if I'd just stepped into a refrigerator. The atmosphere in that room was sure chilly.

"Will someone please tell me what's going on?" I pleaded in total bewilderment.

Brusquely Tracey tossed a newspaper at me. "You mean you don't know about *this*?" she snapped.

The paper was the *City Sun*. My interview! I'd been so busy all day with school and then a modeling job that I hadn't read it. I quickly turned to the middle of the paper where all the TV, movie, and music stuff was. There in bold headline letters I saw CHLOE CHANG A STAR TO WATCH.

Leaning on the sink against the wall, I read the article under the glow of the red bulb.

> Chloe Chang is a vivacious ball of energy. She may be petite, but as soon as you meet her, you can tell she's a big talent. Her dark eyes shine with an inner life and gaze at you with a directness that is a bit unsettling.

"Wow!" I murmured as I read.

"Oh, yeah, she adored you," Ashley grumbled.

> One can't help but think that it must be hard for a girl like Chloe to find friends to match her bright wit and intelligence. Although she claims to have good friends in the world of modeling, which she's been working in since childhood, this reporter wonders. She

says her best friend Ashley Taylor thinks only about modeling. Another friend, model Nikki Wilton, "has never really done anything." Chloe can hardly believe that friend Tracey Morris is even a model. And working for "slave driver" Kate Calico would strain any young girl. One hopes that with her continuing role on "Freshman Bell," this talented girl will move into an area of creativity more suited to her.

I put the paper down in shock. "I never said these things," I told them.

"Oh, she just made it all up?" Nikki asked scornfully. "I've never done anything? Is that what you think of me?"

"That's not what I said," I told her. "I mean, I might have said those words, but she twisted them all around. I was saying that since you became a model, you've traveled and experienced things that you hadn't before."

Nikki turned to me with her hands on her hips. "I might not have jetted around the world, or been to fancy parties, or ridden in limousines and taxis. But I haven't done *nothing!* I've studied gymnastics and flute. I have good friends at school. I've been on vacations with my family. We drove to the Grand Canyon last year. You make me sound like I've just been sitting in front of the TV all my life!"

"That's not how I meant it!" I insisted.

"At least she can believe you're a model," Tracey jumped

in. "Why can't you believe I'm a model, Chloe? What do you think? That I'm not pretty and graceful and dainty enough to be a model? Well, at least I'm not a shrimp."

"Don't call me a shrimp!" I protested. Now *I* was starting to get angry. "For your information, I was giving you a compliment. I was saying that you have a lot of interests and you're not all wrapped up in fashion and hair and stuff like that."

"Oh, you mean the way I am," said Ashley. "Vain, brainless me who only thinks about modeling. And I thought you were my best friend. Boy, was I wrong."

"I was trying to say that you're more sure that you want to be a model than I am. That's all. You're very dedicated to modeling. Isn't that true?"

Ashley folded her arms and turned away. "That's *not* what's printed in the paper."

She was right. It wasn't. I should have chosen my words more carefully. But how could I know how the article would come out?

"Calling Kate a slave driver was really low, too," added Ashley. "She's been nice to you ever since you came to the agency. That's a really great way to repay her."

"I said Kate was the best," I defended myself. "I said some people think she's a slave driver at first."

"Sure you did," Tracey said sarcastically.

"I did!" I shouted, stamping my foot in frustration.

"Tell that to Ms. Calico," Nikki scoffed.

"That's just what I'm going to do," I said, turning toward the door. "Some friends you guys have turned out to be."

"That's funny, coming from a traitor!" Ashley shot back.

"Traitor!" I sputtered. Too angry to say another word, I went out the door and stomped down the hall toward Kate's office.

But when I got there, I hesitated a moment in front of the heavy wooden doors. What exactly was I going to tell Kate? Would she be as angry and unwilling to understand as Ashley, Nikki, and Tracey had been? Was my modeling career over?

All I could do was go inside and try to explain. I raised my hand to knock on the door, but I was interrupted by the sound of a voice.

"She's not in," Kate's assistant, Renata Marco, called to me from her smaller office across the hall from Kate's. She's very pretty and stylish in a gypsy sort of way. Her long hair is curly and blond, and she always wears flowing dresses. She probably could have been a model herself if she wasn't—like me—so petite. "She went out to talk to a client," Renata added. "Are you okay, Chloe?"

I guess my anger and upset were written all over my face. "I've been better," I admitted. "Did you see the *City Sun* today?"

Renata raised her eyebrows and nodded. "Thanks for not mentioning me."

"Well, I would have, but the reporter was asking me questions pretty quickly and—"

"No, it's okay. I'm serious." Renata laughed. "After what you said about the others, I'm glad you didn't mention me."

"Oh, Renata," I sighed. "It all came out wrong! Has Kate seen it?"

"She had the paper tucked under her arm when she left, but I don't know if she's read it or not."

"Just great," I said grimly. A glance at the small clock on Renata's desk told me it was nearly four-thirty. "Oh, no!" I cried. "I'm supposed to be over at 'Freshman Bell' in ten minutes!"

Dashing down the hall, I came out into the front lobby where Michelle was waiting. "Come on," I said, nearly yanking her off the couch.

Down in the street, we were able to hail a cab and get to the studio only five minutes late. As Michelle settled into a folding chair just outside the door, I ran breathlessly into the studio and onto the set. "Sorry, I'm late," I panted.

"That's okay, Chloe," Mr. Mason said pleasantly. "I was just explaining to the cast that we're going to play this like a spoof of detective shows. We'll have lots of funny detective music in the background, and there will be lots of gags, but we want the actors to be dead serious even when they're delivering a joke."

"Okay," I agreed.

He talked to us for another few minutes and then told us to get in place for a run-through of the script. "We'll start from the scene where Scooter finds you," Mr. Mason told me. "Start from the line 'Ah so.' "

"But I thought that was going to change," I said. "Remember? You said you'd talk to the writers."

Mr. Mason looked puzzled, as if he didn't know what I was talking about. Then his eyes lit. "Oh, yes, I talked to them. The writers said they thought the line was a good way to introduce your character. They wanted to leave it in."

As he spoke, his eyes darted around over my head. I remembered what Mom had said about not trusting people who didn't look at you when they spoke. But maybe he was just busy checking out something on the set behind me.

"Well, I'll try it, I guess," I said, wanting to be cooperative. After all, today I'd lost my best friends and I might have lost my modeling career. I couldn't afford to blow this, too.

"It'll be funny. Don't worry," said a skinny boy with lots of curly red hair and freckles. He was Corey Johnson, the actor who played Scooter.

"Get in position," Mr. Mason said. "Chloe, you stand on the yellow X marked on the set floor. Okay?"

I nodded and found the yellow tape crossed in an X in front of one of the set stores. I noticed that a sign had been added to the store. It read: PEKING LAUNDRY. "They call the city Beijing now," I said to Mr. Mason.

"Peking is funnier," Mr. Mason said.

What was funny about Peking? Mr. Mason read my puzzled expression. "We have jokes about *peeking* into the

Peking Laundry," he explained. "Scooter spends a lot of time looking for you, and one of the things he does is peek into the laundry where you work. It's in another scene."

"Oh," I said. I supposed he knew what he was doing. The thought of Grandma working in a laundry so long ago came into my mind. I wondered what her laundry was called. How did it feel to live in a new land, doing very hard work, barely speaking English?

The scene began with Scooter running up to me on the set street. He stretched his arms wide like I was his long-lost friend. My character, Mystery Girl, just looked at him. Then I said my big line. "Ah so."

"Chloe!" Mr. Mason interrupted. "When you do that line, could you step back, put your hands together, and bow a little?"

"Nobody does that," I objected.

"I know, but people will think it's funny."

"They will?" I questioned.

"Yes," Mr. Mason said. "And we want to show that Scooter is deep in another world where people have strange customs he doesn't understand. This would be a quick way to tell the audience all that."

He was the boss.

"Ah so," I said, giving a little bow.

"Don't you know me?" asked the Scooter character.

After he said that line, I was supposed to walk away from him and crash into a garbage can which then knocks over a fruit cart. I was to roll right out of the fall, keep going, and leave Scooter with the mess. That part I had no problem with. It was all the pratfalls in the summer special that had gotten me so much attention.

I started to walk away, but Mr. Mason interrupted again. "Chloe, I think it would be funny if Scooter makes you nervous and you go into a judo position."

"But why would my character know judo? Besides, it should be kung fu."

"Kung fu, judo, whatever," said Mr. Mason. "People associate Asians with martial arts."

"My character is just an average girl," I protested. "All Asians don't know martial arts. I never studied any of it."

"It will be funny," said Mr. Mason. "Really."

"Mr. Mason, I don't feel right doing that," I said.

Mr. Mason came up to me on the set. He put his hand on my shoulder and talked to me in a low, confidential tone. "Chloe, listen. Our idea is to work you in as a series regular. Once you become Scooter's girlfriend, you'll slowly become more and more American. That's why we've made Mystery Girl so Chinese. It gives us a starting point for the development of your character. Don't mention this to the rest of the cast. They don't know yet. You'll be replacing someone who is about to be fired."

Wow! I was going to be a regular. My career as a TV comedian was about to begin!

"All right, sure," I said, feeling dazed.

"Okay, star, let's see the karate stance," said Mr. Mason.

"Kung fu," I corrected him.

"Whatever. Let's see it."

Grandma had taught me a little tai chi chuan, which is more of an exercise than a martial art. It's an ancient art, and people still do it in China today. I assumed the beginning stance and went through a couple of the movements.

"Sorry, Chloe," said Mr. Mason. "It doesn't look right. Couldn't you do something more real-looking?"

"That's really tai chi," I explained. "It can be a martial art at a very advanced level."

"It's not funny," Mr. Mason insisted. "Can you leap in the air and do a karate shout?"

"I suppose," I said.

"Okay, then. Do that."

I'd seen enough martial arts films to fake the move. Then I walked down the pretend street and hit the garbage can, which tumbled over, and knocked down a fruit stand loaded with plastic fruit. The fruit rolled everywhere. Then I went into a forward roll and came right to my feet. I walked off as Scooter cried, "Wait! Wait!" from behind me.

I heard the sound of a single person clapping loudly from beyond the set. Mr. Mason stepped into the light, still clapping. "Wonderful, Chloe, just wonderful!"

"Thank you," I said.

Only I didn't feel wonderful. But what did I have to feel bad about? I was on the verge of stardom.

Chapter Nine

———◆———

The taxi turned the corner near our apartment. Michelle and I were on our way home from the rehearsal, and the sun was beginning to set. A golden glow bounced off the shop windows. The streets were quiet and empty the way they are for a few hours early in the evening. "Could we get out here and walk?" I asked Michelle.

"Do you feel okay?"

"Yeah, I just want to walk."

"Okay," she agreed. She asked the driver to pull over and paid the fare. We got out and walked down the street without talking. "Is something bothering you?" Michelle asked after a few blocks.

"I don't think so," I said. Honestly, I didn't know. I'd just gotten great news. They wanted me as a regular on

"Freshman Bell." Maybe I was still sad about my fight with my friends. And I still had to face Kate. I hoped she didn't believe I'd called her a slave driver for real.

"Maybe you're just tired," said Michelle, putting her hand on my shoulder.

"Maybe," I agreed.

We got home a little after eight. The dinner crowd was starting to thin out. It would stay slow until ten; then the people who'd been to the theaters and the movies would flood in for a late supper. "Michelle, can you help me get some of these dishes out of the way?" Mom said as we walked in the front door of the restaurant.

Michelle began clearing tables, and I did, too. "Don't you have to write your essay?" Mom asked me.

My essay! She was right. "Okay, I'll go do that now," I said.

"How did the rehearsal go?" Mom asked.

"Pretty well, I guess," I told her.

I went through the noisy kitchen where Dad and his assistant cooks were preparing for the next rush. He was so busy he didn't notice me as I went up the stairs to our apartment.

Opening my backpack on the dining room table, I took out a notebook and pen. I had to go upstairs and talk to Grandma before I could write the essay.

But I just couldn't get in the mood to think about the essay. I'd had such a busy day that I needed a moment to relax. My parents were downstairs, so I could probably steal a half hour of TV time without being bugged to do something more productive.

Settling in on the couch, I used the remote to click on the TV. The news came on. I was just about to click to another channel when I heard something that made me freeze.

"A surprising article appeared today in the *City Sun* concerning model and TV actress Chloe Chang," said the anchorwoman, Lois Littman, sitting at her desk.

"Journalist Lisa Waters quoted Ms. Chang making many disparaging remarks about her coworkers at the Calico Modeling Agency. She implied that popular model Ashley Taylor was obsessed with her career. And the talented young model went as far as calling the agency's owner, former supermodel Kate Calico, a slave driver."

"What?" I cried, jumping to my feet.

"Kate Calico, head of the Calico Modeling Agency, declined to comment or to give us Chloe Chang's unlisted number." Lois Littman looked directly into the camera. "Chloe Chang, shame on you."

My jaw dropped. This was unbelievable! I hadn't tried to hurt anyone. Lois Littman made it sound as if I was trying to make myself look good by making my friends look bad. I seemed like a spiteful brat.

My first thought was to call Ashley. That's what I always did when I was upset about something. But Ashley was angry at me. So were Nikki and Tracey.

As I stood wondering what to do, the phone rang. "Hello?" I said, picking up the phone.

"Chloe, dear!" It was Kate Calico. And she'd called me dear. That was a good sign.

"Hi, Kate," I said. "I didn't say you were a slave driver." I got right to the point. "I hope you don't think I did, because I didn't. Honestly. I said some people *thought* you were a slave driver, but you weren't. That whole article came out wrong. I wouldn't want you to think—"

"It's all right, Chloe," Ms. Calico said, cutting me off. "I know how those things happen. I've been misquoted so often, I certainly understand. Besides, it won't stop models from signing with us because we're a fair and reputable agency. And our customers will love it. If I'm a slave driver, it means I work my models hard and the client is getting the most for his or her money."

"Oh, I guess so," I said. I hadn't thought of it that way. "Well, I'm glad you're not mad."

"Absolutely not. No harm done," Kate said. "But that's not why I'm calling. Did you happen to see the news just now?"

"I'm afraid so."

"One little newspaper piece won't do much harm. But with the TV news picking up the story, we want to set the record straight right away. What did you really say about the others?" she asked.

I told her what I'd actually said. "All right," she said calmly. "I figured it was something like that. I'm going to arrange a press conference for you tomorrow. Can you be at the agency by three-thirty?"

"Sure," I agreed. "But I'm supposed to go down to the zoo then and do a photo shoot for Tiger Togs."

"Oh, that's right," Ms. Calico said. "Well, I'll call the Tiger Togs ad agency and have them push back the shoot an hour. We want to clear this up right away. We don't want you to lose modeling bookings because of bad publicity."

"All right," I said. "I'll be there."

As I hung up, I realized I felt a little dizzy. I'd stopped for a hot dog outside the TV studio, but maybe it wasn't enough. I took a banana from the fruit bowl on the dining room table and sat down to eat it.

What a day this had been! So much had happened— good and bad. And there was still so much left to do. I had to talk to Mom and Dad about being a regular on "Freshman Bell." They *had* to say it was all right. They just *had* to! Then tomorrow I would have to talk to a roomful of reporters.

I had to write my essay, too! I decided to take the lazy way out on that one. Mom had told me enough about Grandma. I could do the assignment without talking to her about her life. I was just so tired that all I wanted to do was write it and go to bed.

In my room, I took out some loose-leaf paper and began. *My grandmother was a feminist before she ever heard the word,* I wrote. *She fought her family until they allowed her to study medicine. Grandma told me she wanted to be a doctor from the time she was very small. Her first patients were injured animals. Then one day, her father's carriage broke down as she and her dad were traveling through a poor town. While the carriage was being fixed, Grandma, who was just a girl, saw a healer do an amazing thing.*

Suddenly I didn't feel tired anymore. Writing this essay made me feel better than I'd felt all day. Grandma's life was really interesting. Putting it all down on paper was like writing an adventure tale. Best of all, I didn't have to make up my smart, brave, and kind heroine. She was real. And she was *my* grandmother.

Chapter Ten

———◆———

I walked into Kate Calico's office after school the next day and wanted to run for my life! The office was jammed—and I mean *jammed!*—with reporters and photographers. It made me nervous to talk in front of so many people, especially after what had happened with Lisa Waters.

Feeling panicky, I turned to my mother, who had come with me. The night before, when I'd told my parents what Lois Littman reported on the news, Mom insisted on attending the press conference. I was doubly glad she was there now that I saw how many unfamiliar faces were staring at me.

I'm sure Mom could see the anxious look in my eyes. "Everyone is quite interested in you," she whispered with a small smile. "You're becoming quite a celebrity."

She was right, really. There was no reason to be scared. They were all here to hear my side of the story, after all. Only important people got this kind of reaction from the press.

Taking a deep breath, I calmed down a bit. I put on my best modeling smile and walked into the middle of the room.

"Here she is," said Kate, getting up from behind her wide wooden desk. "This is Chloe Chang and her mother, Donna Chang. They are here to tell you what Chloe really said during the *City Sun* interview." Kate gestured for me to sit in her leather desk chair. She pulled over another chair for Mom.

"Okay, Chloe, what really happened?" asked a reporter.

"Well, you see," I began in a small voice, "I didn't realize that—"

"Louder, please," shouted a reporter in the back of the room.

"I didn't realize," I repeated, nearly shouting. Kate caught my eye as she stood off to the side. Patting the air, she gestured for me to lower my voice. I brought it down a little and described what had actually happened.

"So you're saying Lisa Waters lied?" asked a reporter.

"No," I said firmly. "She made the things I said seem to mean different things than they really meant. She used only part of what I said and somehow she twisted it. I don't know, but—"

"The term is 'out of context,'" Kate cut in. "She took Chloe's words out of their proper context. I'm sure you're all familiar with how that can happen."

A murmur of agreement spread through the reporters. They nodded and smiled as they jotted notes or held up small tape recorders.

"Was Lisa Waters deliberately trying to make you look bad?" another reporter asked.

"My daughter is not a mind reader." Mom spoke up, adding, "She can't know what Ms. Waters intended. I suggest you ask Ms. Waters these sorts of questions."

With a quick glance, I saw that Kate was smiling and nodding at my mother.

"Will you be a regular on 'Freshman Bell'?" a short man on my left asked.

I remembered that Mr. Mason had told me not to tell. Besides, I hadn't told my parents about this yet. "I'm not sure what will happen," I replied.

"Have you gotten a reaction from the models mentioned in the article?" asked a woman reporter.

"They were very angry but I tried to explain that I didn't say those things the way they sounded," I said. "I feel very badly that their feelings were hurt because they're my friends—at least they *were* my friends before that article came out. And Kate Calico is *not* a slave driver."

"It's all right, Chloe. Sometimes I am," Ms. Calico said with laughter in her voice. "But Chloe didn't tell that to the reporter. Chloe is a forthright and honest girl. The Calico Modeling Agency is proud to have her as one of our junior models. We stand by her one hundred percent."

I smiled at Kate. She really was the best!

"Now, if you'll excuse us," said Kate. "Chloe has a modeling job she must get to. Thank you all so much for coming. We know you'll print only what's fair and true."

Slowly the reporters filed out of Kate's office. "I think that went very well," said Kate, joining Mom and me.

Mom patted my hand. "I was proud of you, Chloe."

"Thanks, Mom," I replied.

"That was a good response on the Lisa Waters issue," Kate said to Mom. "Let them ask her themselves. We don't want her suing us for making false accusations. The reporter only asked that question hoping to stir up more trouble."

"Why?" I asked.

Kate smiled sadly. "More trouble means more juicy stories to sell more papers and magazines."

"We'd better be getting a taxi to the zoo," Mom told me.

"If you don't mind, I'd like to take Chloe myself," said Kate.

"Why?" I asked.

Kate went to the window and pulled aside the drapes. "See for yourself."

Mom and I looked way down to the street. A bunch of kids around my age were crowded together by the front door. "Who are they?" I asked.

"Your fans," Kate reported.

"Are you kidding?" I asked, shocked.

Kate shook her head. "Renata checked it out. Those kids are waiting for you. Somehow word got around that you were holding a press conference today. They came to get a look at you and to have you sign autographs."

"How do they even know about me?" I questioned.

" 'Kids Talk!' is a very popular show. And you were a headline on the news last night. A lot of them liked you in the 'Freshman Bell' special, too," Kate explained.

"Wow," I said softly. I hadn't expected this.

"Come on, we'll go down the fire stairs," said Kate. "My limo is waiting there. Shall we drop you at home, Donna?"

"No, I'll take a cab," said Mom. "I know she's in good hands as long as you're with her, Kate."

Mom left and Kate and I went down the back stairs. We climbed into the long black limo with its dark tinted glass. We could see out, but no one could see in. We drove right past the kids as they stood outside the agency door. "It seems sort of mean just to leave them standing there," I commented.

"I asked Renata to tell them you'd left," said Kate. "If we'd stopped for them, you'd never have gotten to your shoot on time."

"It's all so weird," I said. "I'm the same person, but suddenly everyone is interested in me."

"You're becoming a celebrity. How does it feel?"

"I don't know yet," I said honestly. "In a way, it's very exciting. I mean, I don't think I have much future as a fashion model, and I don't want to become just a regular kid who goes to school. I've always worked and I want to keep doing it. This solves all my problems."

Kate smiled, but her smile was a little sad. "Don't let life run you, Chloe. You run it."

"What do you mean?"

"You call the shots. You do what you think is right, and you try for what you want. If you truly want to be a fashion model, go for it. Don't just say, 'Oh, I'm too short.' Try to convince clients that small is great. If you can't, at least you've tried."

"Don't you have to be realistic?" I asked.

"Yes," said Kate. "But you can define what is realistic. You don't always have to follow other people's rules. When I started out as a model, everyone thought I was just a pretty young woman with no mind. When my modeling career was winding down, people told me I should become an actress. But I had no talent for acting. I made a few awful movies which made that pretty clear. Yet, despite what anyone thought or said, *I* knew I could run a business."

"I think maybe I *could* be a comedian," I said.

"Then do it your way. You're a strong, bright girl, Chloe. If you follow your instincts, you'll be fine."

I nodded thoughtfully. Kate made it sound easy. But I

wasn't so sure it was.

We arrived at the zoo and walked quickly to the tiger area. The photographer and Andrea Marcus, the representative from Tiger Togs, were waiting for us. I changed into a tiger-print jumpsuit in the zoo's rest room.

The Tiger Togs ad people had talked the zoo people into feeding the tigers near the front of their enclosure. That way we would be able to get them in the picture. The photographer had me stand on a blue wooden box in front of them. "Gaze over at the tigers as if you're dying to get into that moat area with them," the photographer instructed me.

"We want to get across the idea that wearing Tiger Togs makes you feel like a tiger," added Andrea. "Hey, I know!" She ran over to a vendor and bought a hamburger. Handing it to me, she said, "Pretend to eat this. We can call this ad 'Feeding Time for Tigers.' I love it!"

I did my best to look tigerish as I looked at the tigers and pretended to bite into the hamburger. They were really beautiful animals, so strong and self-assured. Behind them, an artificial waterfall sprayed down some rocks. As zoo habitats went, it was an awfully nice one. But it reminded me of the "Freshman Bell" set. It wasn't the real thing. I wondered if the tigers knew the difference.

The photographer was very fussy. He wanted everything just right. "Turn to the left," he said. "Now hold the hamburger higher. A little higher. Perfect."

As I stood with my hamburger raised, I became aware of a strange sound. It was almost like a dull drumming. Then, with a jolt, I realized what the sound was. It was my name. Voices were chanting my name over and over.

I turned sharply. "You moved!" the photographer cried.

Behind me, about thirty kids were being held in back of a barricade by zoo security. "Chloe! Chloe!" they chanted. When they saw I was looking at them, they started waving autograph books. "Chloe, sign my book." "Chloe, sign my hand!" "Sign my T-shirt!" I heard them shout.

"Go over for just a minute," said Ms. Calico.

"I have a shoot to do," Andrea complained.

"Don't you want a star representing your client?" asked Kate. "The next time, you might have to pay more to get Chloe Chang to represent your company. Much more."

"Oh, all right," the rep sighed.

I went over to the kids and began signing stuff a mile a minute. "We love you, Chloe!" called a girl who looked about nine. Behind her, two other girls waved their autograph books at me. "We do, we love you!" they shouted.

"Thanks," I said, smiling at them. It's nice to be loved, but how could they love me? They didn't even know me.

"Chloe, marry me!" said a cute boy of about twelve.

I laughed and signed a piece of paper he handed me. This was getting really crazy!

Chapter Eleven

By the time I got home that evening, I was pooped. I plopped facedown right on the living room couch. Fumbling around on the coffee table, I found the remote and clicked on the TV. I was hoping to see something about my press conference. Instead, I saw myself at the zoo.

Then the scene switched to a woman reporter standing in front of the monkey cage. "Despite the *City Sun* article, Chloe Chang's fans remain loyal," the reporter said into her microphone. "At a press conference today, Chloe claimed that her comments about fellow models were taken out of context, and she regretted the pain they had caused. Her fans apparently believe her. Today they mobbed the rising star at the zoo. Chloe mania has hit, and no one knows where it will end. It is rumored that the young model-turned-comedian is on the verge of signing a major recording contract. Tune in at eleven for today's press conference with Chloe Chang. This is Rita Ryman, reporting from the zoo."

"Recording contract!" I yelped. Where had she gotten that story? Chloe mania? What was that supposed to mean?

At that moment, the phone rang. The cordless phone wasn't on its base, which wasn't unusual at our apartment. After two rings, it stopped ringing. Someone must have answered it.

I was still thinking about the TV report when my brother Matt came in from his bedroom carrying the phone. "Oh, you *are* home," he said. "I didn't think you were. That was some guy named Dave Davis. He wants to offer you a recording contract."

"What?" I cried. "I can't sing."

"I told him that," said Matt. "He said it didn't matter. He says you're hot, and Zany Records wants to snap you up before anyone else does. He gave me these phone numbers." He handed me a piece of paper with four numbers written on it.

"Well, which one is his number?" I asked.

"All of them," Matt replied. "One is his office phone. The others are his home phone, his car phone, and the cellular phone he carries with him."

"Wow," I said. "He must really want to talk to me. Give me the phone, please."

Matt handed me the phone and sat on the edge of the couch while I punched in the numbers. The receptionist put me through to Dave Davis right away. "Chloe, sweetheart," he said. "I'm glad you called me right back. Your brother says you sing like a dying moose. Is that true?"

"I wouldn't put it that way," I said. "But I don't think I'm much of a singer."

"No problem," said Mr. Davis. "I'll have to contact your agent, of course."

"I don't have one. You'll have to talk to my mom and dad."

"Tell them to call me anytime, day or night. We want to move on this as soon as possible."

"All right," I said. "Thank you very much. I'm sure they'll call you right away. Bye."

Just then Mom came in, holding Amanda. "Who was that?" she asked.

"Chloe is going to be a rock star," said Matt excitedly. "She was just offered a record deal."

Mom frowned. "Really?"

I nodded as I hopped off the couch. "He has to talk to you and Dad." I held the phone out to her. "Can you please call him now?"

"Is this something you want to do?" Mom asked as she set Amanda down and let her toddle around the room.

"Sure it is!" I said. "Who wouldn't?"

"But do you think you really have a talent for singing?" Mom asked.

"Dave Davis says it doesn't matter," I replied. "He should know about stuff like that. It's his business."

"I suppose," said Mom. "Still, I wonder if it's an area where you really shine."

Now I was getting bugged at her. "Some people believe in me," I snapped.

"Chloe," Mom said sternly, "I believe in you completely. I just don't think singing is one of your greatest talents."

"Mom, this is my big chance to be a rock star," I insisted.

"I never heard you say you wanted to be a rock star," Mom argued.

"Wake up, Mom," said Matt. "Everybody wants to be a rock star."

"Oh, I didn't know that," Mom replied, still sounding doubtful. "Well, let me talk to your father."

"What's there to talk about?" I asked anxiously. "He's got to say yes."

"We'll let you know after we talk," said Mom. "I know you're excited but you'll just have to wait. Sorry, honey."

"Oh, all right," I mumbled, my shoulders sagging. What choice did I have?

"Now I have to give Amanda her bath," she said. She scooped Amanda up and went down the hall.

I turned to Matt. "They'll say yes, won't they?"

Matt shrugged. "Who can tell with Dad?" he said. That was true. I loved my dad, but he had his own ideas about how things should be. He was strict in some ways and very easygoing in others. It was hard to predict what he would say.

I wanted to call Ashley. What good was having great things happen to you if you didn't get to share them with your friends, especially your best friend? I'd expected to hear from at least one of them by now. But I guess they didn't miss me. They were doing just fine without me.

Suddenly it felt as if my fingers had a mind of their own. They started punching in Ashley's phone number. I hadn't decided I wanted to call her, but my fingers had.

"Hello?" Ashley answered.

"Um . . . uh . . ." I stammered.

"Chloe, is that you?" Ashley demanded.

"No Chloe here," I answered. "You have the wrong number."

"Hey, you called me!" I heard her shout as I clicked off the phone. I sat with the phone in my lap. I really missed Ashley.

By later that night, Mom and Dad had talked. They said yes! "But I'll be watching your grades," Dad warned. "At the slightest drop, something will have to go."

"I understand, Dad," I said, hugging him. "I'll work really hard at school. You'll see."

"I'm serious, Chloe," Dad said.

"I know. Really, I know. You won't be sorry."

Dad nodded. "I hope not."

The very next morning, a big envelope arrived by messenger. In it was a contract for Mom and Dad to read. There were also two songs for me to learn, along with a cassette tape with the music on it.

I ran to my room and put on the tape. The music was really peppy and lively. I read the words to the songs. One was called "Lollipop Love." The other was "Boy of My Dreams."

The words weren't hard to remember. "Your love is sweet as lollipops, lollipops, lollipops, love. Oooh, oooh, oooh. Lollipop love." How hard was that? About as hard as saying "Ah so."

Actually, both songs were pretty dumb. Oh, well. When I was a bigger star, I could demand better songs. Maybe I could even write my own.

I spent the afternoon standing on my bed so I could see my whole self in my bedroom mirror. I sang the songs at the top of my lungs as the cassette played along.

"Are you in pain?" my brother Tommy shouted into the room.

"Very funny!" I shouted back, unamused.

"Well, I am," he said. "Do you have to sing so loud?"

I hopped off the bed and slammed the door in his face. Dave Davis said I'd be fine. I didn't need my family telling me I wouldn't be.

Just as I was rewinding the cassette, there was a knock on my door. "Dad wants you to come down and help out front," Michelle called.

"Okay," I answered through the door. I snapped off the cassette, but somehow I didn't want to go. I had too many exciting things happening to want to be clearing tables.

Maybe when I was a big star, I'd be so rich that my family wouldn't have to run a restaurant. They could sell it. Or I could hire people to run it for them. I'd pay all Michelle's medical school bills and send my brother to chef school in Paris. Mom could rest. Dad could . . . I don't know. What would he do if he didn't have the restaurant? He'd figure something out.

"Chloe!" Michelle yelled.

"Okay, okay," I grumbled. "I'm coming."

Chapter Twelve

Can you see me after class, Chloe?" Mrs. Elmont asked during Monday's English class.

Right away, my heart started to thump. "Sure," I said, worried. Had my essay been *that* bad? I knew I'd written it fast, but it had just sort of come spilling out of me. And even though I hadn't talked to Grandma, I had talked to Mom. I knew enough to write it.

I sat through class and barely heard a word Mrs. Elmont said. I was too worried to pay attention. I didn't need a school problem now, not with Dad watching my grades like a hawk. Something like this could cause him to call Dave Davis right back and say he'd changed his mind. He hadn't signed the contract yet.

After class, I waited while the other kids filed out. "You wanted to see me," I said, going to Mrs. Elmont's desk.

"Yes, Chloe. It's about your essay. I—"

"I'll do it over," I jumped in. "I know it was late to begin with and I know you had to start with a B, but if I get any lower than a B, I'm dead meat. Maybe not quite dead meat, of course, but pretty close. I mean, it would ruin my life and—"

"Chloe, Chloe, hold on," said Mrs. Elmont with a soft laugh. "The essay was great. I liked it. In fact, I loved it."

"You did?" I was surprised.

"Yes. I liked it so much that I'd like to enter it in the district essay contest."

A wide smile crossed my face. "That would really impress my dad," I said.

Mrs. Elmont smiled back. "I'm sure it would. Only five essays from each school can be submitted. It's an honor even to enter."

"Could you write my dad a letter telling him that?" I requested.

"Is there a problem at home?" Mrs. Elmont asked.

"Oh, no," I assured her. "It's just that Dad worries about my grades, what with everything happening with my career and all."

"I saw you on the news," said Mrs. Elmont. "It does sound as if you're quite busy these days with all the . . . uh . . . Chloe mania."

"Yeah, Chloe mania," I said. "It's pretty funny, huh?"

"I'm sure it's very exciting," said Mrs. Elmont. "I'd be

98

glad to write your father. In the meantime, I'd like you to do a little more work on this essay. All you really need are some direct quotes from your grandmother. Since you're lucky enough to have her live so close, just ask her a few questions."

"Sure thing," I said, taking the essay from her. "How long do I have to work on this?"

Mrs. Elmont frowned. "The deadline for all submissions is tomorrow. I know it's not much notice, but if you'd been on time originally, I would have—"

"I understand," I broke in. "I'll talk to Grandma tonight and have it in to you tomorrow." I wasn't going to let such a good chance to impress Dad slip away.

"Very good. I'll look forward to seeing it," Mrs. Elmont said.

I was feeling good as I stepped out into the hallway. A group of seventh-grade girls rushed up to me. "Chloe, we can't believe you actually go to our school," said a redhead with braces. "Please sign my book."

I smiled and signed it. Then I signed seven more books and six pieces of loose-leaf, plus two copies of a Little Princess catalog with my picture in it. "My mother says I should keep this because it will be worth money some day," said a thin blonde girl, clutching the catalog. "When I go home, I'll put this in a freezer bag right away."

Kids were keeping pictures of me in freezer bags? How strange. I saw more kids coming my way, but I knew I'd be late for my next class if I signed any more autographs. "Sorry, I've got to get to class," I told them, waving my hand as I hurried down the hall.

I needed my science notebook, so I stopped at my locker before going to class. The girl whose locker was next to mine, Allison Wyman, had her door open, so she didn't see me come up to my locker from the opposite side. Although we don't have any classes together, I usually say hi to her, and we talk a little every day. I was about to say something to her when I heard her talking to someone. "Did you see the way she was signing autographs in the hall?" Allison said.

I froze. She could only be talking about me.

"I know, like she was a big deal or something," agreed the other girl, whose voice I didn't recognize.

"Now she thinks she's too good for everyone. She doesn't even speak to me anymore. She's become totally stuck-up!" said Allison.

Stuck-up! I hadn't talked to Allison in a few days simply because I hadn't seen her. What was she talking about?

Allison slammed her locker shut. "Oh, Chloe," she stammered when she saw me. Beside her was a girl I'd seen around but didn't know. "How long have you been standing there?"

"Long enough to hear how you feel about me," I said.

"Don't flatter yourself," said Allison. "The whole world isn't talking about *you.*"

"But you were," I insisted. "I haven't become stuck-up."

Allison looked embarrassed and laughed nervously. "Well, you know how it is with Chloe mania. I suppose you can't help it. It's really not your fault. See ya."

I was stunned. What wasn't my fault? How had I acted stuck-up?

For the rest of the day, I was very aware of not acting stuck-up. I smiled and waved at everyone I knew. But things had changed. At lunchtime I went to sit with the kids I usually sit with, but they acted differently toward me. One girl, Angela, wouldn't even look at me, except when she thought I wasn't paying attention.

Another girl acted as if she had to be my servant. "Can I bring your tray back for you?" she asked toward the end of lunch.

"No, I can do it myself," I said, making extra sure to say it pleasantly.

She actually tugged my tray out of my hands. "No, let me. Stars shouldn't be getting messed up with cafeteria food."

It was really weird. Even Tony, a guy I always joke around with, didn't blow a straw wrapper at me or try to put an ice cube down my back or anything.

I usually walked home from school with some kids who live near me. But when I got to the doorway where we usually meet, I saw they had already headed off. I guess they figured I was too big a star to want to walk with them anymore.

After a few blocks, I ran into a group of fifth graders from the elementary school around the corner. "Chloe!" one of them cried. It was a boy I'd never seen before. The next thing I knew, I was surrounded by fifth graders wanting to shake my hand and have me sign autographs. One fifth-grade boy even asked me to kiss him! I blew him a kiss.

By the time I got home, I was in a pretty bad mood. The only good thing that had happened was the essay. But that meant I'd have to hurry up and revise it.

"Chloe," said Michelle as I walked into the kitchen, "Dave Davis from the record company called. He wants you to go there to start recording."

"When?" I asked.

"At four-thirty."

"Today?"

Michelle nodded. "He said you knew Zany Records was in a hurry to get started, so you'd understand."

"Wow! This is all happening so fast," I said. "I suppose I could be there." Just then, Dad came into the kitchen from the restaurant. "Dad, may I go to Zany Records today? It's just ten blocks uptown from here."

Dad's eyes flashed to the clock on the wall. "Michelle, can you go with her?"

"I guess so," Michelle said.

"All right, but I don't want either of you there later than nine o'clock. If you stay later than seven, take a cab home.

And remember, I haven't signed that contract yet. If you see anything you don't like, let me know."

"Okay," I agreed. Then I went upstairs, showered, and put on a pair of black-and-white-striped leggings, a black tunic top, bright red socks, and my white canvas high-tops.

Michelle and I were just about to leave when the phone rang. "Ignore it," I told Michelle. I was anxious to get going.

The phone stopped ringing. As I was closing the door behind me, Matt came out into the living room. "Chloe, it's for you," he called.

"Who is it?"

"Ashley."

Ashley. My heart thumped. I had to see what she wanted. "Just a minute," I told Michelle.

"Hello," I said, taking the phone from Matt.

"That was you on the phone the other day, wasn't it?" Ashley said. She was her usual blunt self.

"Well," I hesitated, not knowing what was coming next. "Well, yes, it was. So what? I . . . I misdialed."

"You did not." Ashley laughed. "You miss me as much as I miss you."

"You do? Miss me, I mean?"

"Of course I do, even though I was totally furious at you. You really hurt my feelings, you know."

"I didn't say those things the way they sounded!" I exploded, frustrated that she couldn't seem to understand that.

"I know. I know," she muttered. "Kate and I had this big talk. She told me all about how she and her husband almost got divorced because of something someone wrote. She'd said he was more artistic than ambitious, and the reporter wrote that Kate said he was a big loser."

"How terrible," I sympathized.

"She said it was awful," said Ashley. "Anyway, she got me to see how stuff like that could happen. Want me to come over? I think we should talk."

"Chloe," Michelle called. "Hurry up."

"I can't," I said. "I have to go to Zany Records. They offered me a recording contract."

Ashley squealed so loudly that I had to hold the phone away from my ear. Suddenly everything seemed real and wonderful again.

"I'll meet you there," she said. "These record types are very tricky. You need me to watch out for you."

"All right," I said. "Come on."

Ashley was back, and I felt happier than I had in days!

Chapter Thirteen

---◆---

What key would you like to sing in?" the synthesizer player asked me. I was in a Zany Records recording studio with him and three women who were backup singers.

The studio had a big panel of glass dividing it from the sound booth on the other side. The sound booth had so many lights and dials and levers that it looked like we were on the bridge of the starship *Enterprise*.

What key did I want? Who knew? Not me. I had no idea about keys. I shrugged, feeling stupid. "I don't know."

"E," I heard Ashley say from the sound booth. Her voice was amplified by a round microphone built into the glass. "She wants the key of E."

"What are you, her agent?" asked Dave Davis, a short man in a wild Hawaiian print shirt who was in the sound booth with Ashley and Michelle. He was bald on top, but he'd combed the hair from the side of his head over the bald spot to cover it.

"Maybe I am," Ashley shot back.

"Excuse me," I said. I walked up to the glass and spoke to them through it. "Can I talk to you a minute, Ashley?"

Mr. Davis looked annoyed. "All right, come into the sound booth. But just for a second. I'm paying these musicians by the hour."

I walked through the door and pulled Ashley over to one side. "Why do I want the key of E?" I whispered.

"I don't know," Ashley whispered back. "I always hear people say that on TV shows and all."

"Ashley, I can't do this," I said. "I don't know what I'm doing."

"Of course you do," Ashley insisted. "Just don't let them push you around." Ashley turned toward Mr. Davis. "You know, my client hasn't signed a contract yet. She's doing you a favor just by being here."

Mr. Davis turned red at the temples. "Please get back out there," he said to me in a voice that barely masked his impatience.

I returned to the studio. The musician at the synthesizer began to play. It sounded like an entire orchestra was coming out of that one instrument. "Remember, Chloe, we just want to get a feel for your voice," Mr. Davis said through the microphone. "Then we'll lay down the instrumentals and the backup tracks. You can come in another time, and we'll get your vocal track down."

Earlier, Mr. Davis had explained to me about tracks. I didn't understand it entirely. It seemed that they didn't record a song all at once. They recorded the music and the backgrounds, and then the main voices, separately. That way, they could adjust the different sounds to get just the effect they wanted. "That's why it doesn't matter if you can sing or not," Mr. Davis explained to me. "We'll just drown you out with background vocals and instruments."

"Then why would anyone want a record of me singing?" I questioned.

"Because you're you, sweetie pie," he said. "And you're the one they love."

"Oh, I get it," I said. Except that I didn't, really. But I figured he knew what he was talking about.

Now I would have to sing in front of everyone. Up in the booth, Mr. Davis signaled me to start.

"Your love is sweet as lollipops, lollipops, lollipops, love," I sang. At first I felt that things were going pretty well. Maybe I was a better singer than I'd thought. Then I looked at the faces of everyone around me. They weren't exactly smiling and swaying to the beat. Their faces looked more as if they were suffering great pain. Was I *that* bad?

I kept singing, but my voice began to die out as I lost confidence. Up in the booth, Mr. Davis motioned me to keep singing. He seemed to be pushing something up, so I took that to mean he wanted more volume.

Singing louder made it sound better to me. I hoped that if I belted out the song, I might be able to make up for being off-key. When I was finally done, I looked at the booth to see people's reaction.

Mr. Davis leaned toward the microphone in the glass. "Like I said, Chloe, we'll drown you out. I don't think we need you anymore today."

I trudged out of the room feeling totally humiliated. "Was I horrible?" I asked Ashley.

Ashley looked at Michelle. "Yes," said Michelle.

I nodded sadly.

"But, look," Ashley said cheerfully, "you still have a recording contract, so who cares?"

Mr. Davis came over and put his hand on my shoulder. "Chloe, it was fine. This album will sell, and that's all Zany Records cares about. I've called a limo to drop you and your sister and your . . . uh . . . agent here home. I'll see you tomorrow."

"I have to be on the 'Freshman Bell' set tomorrow," I said.

"Day after?" Mr. Davis asked. "Four o'clock?"

"I think that's okay," I said.

Mr. Davis patted my shoulder. "See you then. And don't worry about a thing. This record will be a winner. Leave it all to me."

Michelle and I rode uptown with Ashley in the limousine. "Thanks for coming today," I told her. "Are Nikki and Tracey still mad at me?"

"They haven't had any jobs in the past few days, so I haven't seen them," Ashley said. "I'm going to call them tonight, though. I'll tell them what Kate told me."

"Thanks," I said. "I miss them, too."

Ashley got out of the limo at her fancy apartment building. The doorman held the front door open for her as she waved good-bye.

On the way back downtown, Michelle checked her slim black watch. It was almost eight. "I have so much studying to do tonight," she said.

"Oh, no!" I cried. "I still have my essay to do."

When we were home, I grabbed a small tape recorder from my room, then ran up to Grandma and Grandpa's apartment. "Hello, Flower," said Grandma, answering my knock at the door. "Come in. I hear you are very busy these days becoming a big celebrity."

"Things are pretty exciting," I admitted.

"Does it make you happy?"

What kind of question was that? I didn't know how to answer it. "I suppose," I said.

"Why is that a difficult question?" Grandma asked, as if she'd read my mind.

"Because *happy* is sort of a weird word," I said. "How can you tell if you're happy?"

"Are you filled with joy? Does the world seem like a good and wonderful place to live in? Does your heart tell you that you are on your true path?"

"My heart?" I asked. "My true path?"

Grandma nodded.

"Well, I don't know," I confessed. "I guess I'm happy about it. Who wouldn't be?"

"I don't know," said Grandma. Just then Grandpa came into the living room. Grandpa looks like the oldest man alive. He's small and all wrinkled. He doesn't talk much, but he gave me a little wave as he shuffled by. I waved back.

Grandma spoke to him in Chinese. She seemed to be scolding him as she ushered him back to bed. Then she got him what he'd come out for, a glass of water.

While she was gone, I thought about what she'd said. My heart didn't seem to be in the habit of speaking to me. I always listened to my brain, but not my heart. What sorts of things did a heart say to a person? I tried to hear my heart beating, but I couldn't even hear that.

Grandma returned and sat on the couch. "He thinks he bothers me too much, so he tries to do things for himself. But he should really rest. He's no bother."

"You love Grandpa a lot," I observed.

"Your Grandpa was so strong and bold when he was younger," Grandma said fondly. "I wish you'd known him then. He walked into the laundry one day, and I fell in love with him right away. We were married within six months."

Grandma smiled at the memory. "I was so old that I didn't think I'd ever marry. Funny, now twenty-nine seems so young."

"Did you keep working in the laundry after you married?" I asked her.

"Only for another six months," Grandma replied. "Grandpa encouraged me to go to adult education at night. First I learned English. Then I began working as an aide in the local health center. There were many new Chinese immigrants. I translated for the American doctors. The work was easier and much more interesting than doing laundry."

"Are you sad that you never became a doctor?" I asked.

Grandma looked thoughtful. "Not really. I always knew that my path lay in healing. Through the years, I've learned a lot about the Eastern and the Western ways of healing. Both have something to offer. I would have attained more riches if I'd been a doctor, but that wasn't the important thing to me. I grew up with wealth. I knew it didn't buy happiness. Finding your purpose in life and following it brings happiness. I feel I've done that."

Suddenly I remembered my essay. "Can I record what we're talking about for my essay?" I asked.

Grandma looked a little startled, but she nodded. "I'm honored that you're writing about me."

"You've had the most interesting life of anyone I know," I said, turning on the recorder.

We spoke for almost an hour. She told me all about her life as a girl. She'd had everything she wanted, even a private tutor, like Ashley has. In China at that time, only wealthy people attended school. Girls were permitted to learn to read and write, but that was about all, so Grandma really had to fight her parents for every bit of education she got. When they let her go to medical school, it was a big scandal in her town. But Grandma came back and helped some of the women in the poorer towns deliver their babies. Those people really loved her.

It seemed unfair that just when she'd won that victory, the Communists came into power. A lot of her friends were forced to move to other places and do other jobs than the ones they'd studied for. "It was called relocation, and it was supposed to be for the good of the state," Grandma explained. "But when people are heartbroken because they are pulled away from their homes and the jobs they love, I don't see how the state can benefit. Miserable people make a miserable world." Grandma's family left China rather than be relocated or imprisoned or worse. Still, she never got back to medical school.

She told me how Grandpa and she moved to northern California when Grandpa got a job with a train line. When he retired, they moved here to help Mom and Dad with the restaurant.

All the while, Grandma took care of her children and found ways to be involved with medicine. She worked as a clerk in a pharmacy. She was an assistant to a specialist in acupuncture, which is the practice of relieving pain by putting needles in different parts of the body. And one time when she couldn't find a job, she began growing herbs in her garden and selling them. People bought them for cooking, but they also bought them for healing. Grandma began reading more and more about healing with herbs so she could answer their questions.

"Wow, Grandma, you've had so many changes in your life," I commented. "You were rich, you were poor, you landed in a strange country. You went from studying to be a doctor to working in a laundry. How did you handle all those changes?"

I think that as I asked that question, I was thinking of all the recent changes in my own life. I truly needed to hear her answer.

"There really weren't any changes," Grandma said.

"What?" I asked.

"The world around me changed. But I was always me. No change."

"Didn't the things that happened to you change you?" I asked.

Grandma shook her head slowly. "I grew, perhaps. I learned new things. But the basic person I was never changed. I always tried to do what my heart told me."

"I don't understand how that works," I said. "How do you hear what your heart is saying?"

"You find a quiet place and you listen. If you listen long and patiently with a true desire to know, your heart will speak to you."

Grandma stood up and ruffled the top of my hair. "I'm pretty tired now, Chloe. Do you have enough for your essay?"

"I think so," I said, snapping off the recorder. "Thanks."

"You're very welcome, Flower. I'll see you in the morning."

"Good night, Grandma." I went downstairs and got right to work on my essay. Like the first time, the words came pouring out of me. I ended with what she'd said about listening to her heart, even though I didn't really understand it.

By the time I was done, I was exhausted. I said good night to my parents and then went straight to bed. But I couldn't sleep.

I lay there thinking about everything Grandma and I had talked about. Was I really happy with everything that was happening to me? Did it fill me with joy?

I'm not sure exactly when I drifted off to sleep. The last thing I remember was lying very still in the dark. I was listening—waiting to hear if my heart had anything to say.

Chapter Fourteen

———◆———

Ah so," I said the next day on the "Freshman Bell" set. *Ah so.* The words echoed in my brain. A picture came into my head. I thought of Grandma as a young woman. I'd seen old photos of her from when she'd just arrived in America. She was proud and beautiful. She helped people. I was sure she never bowed and said, "Ah so."

I turned to Mr. Mason. "Can't we please change that line?" I asked.

"Chloe, we've been through this. It's really funny," said Mr. Mason.

"I think it's part of a stereotype," I insisted. "I just don't feel comfortable with it."

Mr. Mason rolled his eyes. "Can we talk about this afterward? Just move ahead to the karate stuff."

"I'd rather not do that, either," I said.

"What are you talking about?" asked Mr. Mason, sounding just a bit angry. "I'm on a deadline here, Chloe. I don't have time for a lot of discussion."

"I'm sorry, Mr. Mason," I said. "Just one more thing. I don't want to do that scene about noodles in the pizzeria."

"Why not?" Mr. Mason asked with an exasperated sigh.

"Because it's not true to life and it's insulting to Chinese people. So are the love potion and the crazy laundry computer."

There was silence on the set. Mr. Mason ran his hand across his cheek. Then he walked onto the set. "Chloe, I appreciate your concerns," he said, bending over close to me and talking in a low voice. "But you're a child and you're new to this business. Believe me, we know what works. We don't want to insult anyone. We just want to make a comedy that people will laugh at."

"What people will laugh?" I asked. "And who will they be laughing at?" Even I was surprised by my words. I hadn't planned to do or say any of this. But the words were coming out of me, and I felt good about saying them.

Mr. Mason leaned over even closer. "Chloe, I don't have time for this. If you can't do it the way it's written, I'll have to replace you."

I heard my heart for sure right then. It felt like it slammed into my rib cage and stopped beating. Replace me? "Mr. Mason, I don't want you to replace me, but I can't do the scene the way it is now," trembling slightly.

Mr. Mason folded his arms. "It's your choice, "You *can* be replaced."

"Then I guess that's what you'll have to do," I said. My knees felt like jelly, but I walked out of the light and away from the set. My hands quivered as I picked my jacket off a folding chair and went out the door.

As I stepped into the hallway, I heard a familiar voice. "Chloe!" It was Ashley. Nikki and Tracey were with her.

They hurried to me and then stopped short. "What happened?" Ashley gasped. "You look like you're about to faint."

Small black dots floated in the air in front of me. "I do feel dizzy," I admitted. "I need a chair."

Tracey slid a metal chair across the hall and I sat down, putting my head between my knees. In a few minutes, I felt more clearheaded. "What are you guys doing here?" I asked as I lifted my head.

"We were coming to make up," said Nikki. "I'm sorry I got so angry at you. Ashley helped me understand how something like what you said could come out wrong."

"Yeah," Tracey agreed. "I'm sorry, too. You're too good a friend to lose over nothing. I can hardly believe I'm a model myself. Why should I get mad at you for saying it?"

"Are you getting the flu or something like that?" Ashley asked me.

I shook my head. "No. I think I just shocked myself, that's all."

"What did you do?" asked Nikki.

"I quit."

"You did *what?*" Ashley screamed.

"Quit," I said. "I didn't intend to. But I just couldn't take all the Chinese stereotypes. I felt like I was betraying myself and my family, especially Grandma. I only realized I felt that way today. Maybe it was the talk I had with Grandma last night. I don't know why the words came out of me, but I know they were right."

My friends were quiet a moment. It seemed they could hardly believe what I'd just told them.

Finally Tracey spoke. "Good for you," she said.

"I agree," said Nikki. "Good for you."

"It sure took guts," said Ashley thoughtfully. "I don't know if I could have done that, but I admire you for it. And, hey, it will give you more time to work on your album. I hope they still want you now that you're not on the show. I know, get your mom and dad to sign that contract real fast before Dave Davis finds out."

"It doesn't matter whether they still want me or not," I said. "I'm not making the album."

"Why not?" asked Nikki.

"Because I can't sing," I said honestly.

Boy, was I ever surprising myself! It seemed that when you listened to your heart, your whole world could fly apart.

It didn't matter, though. My heart was filled with joy, and I felt that the world was once again a wonderful place. I was happy.

I stood up and hugged Nikki and Tracey. "I'm so glad we're friends again," I said sincerely.

"Me, too," said Nikki, hugging back.

"Me, three," added Tracey, squeezing my shoulder.

Michelle came down the hall looking for me. "Are you all right?" she asked. "Mr. Mason told me you quit."

I nodded. "I didn't like the lines."

Michelle smiled. "I didn't, either. Do you want to go home?"

"Could I go out with these guys for a little while?"

"Just be home by dinnertime." Michelle kissed my cheek and walked away.

My friends and I left the TV studio and headed for a nearby diner. We ordered fries and shakes. Four girls at another booth asked for my autograph. I signed their paper place mats, wondering if I'd miss all the attention once Chloe mania died out. In a way, I would. But I wouldn't miss saying lines I didn't feel good about, or pretending I could sing when I couldn't.

When I got home, I told my parents what had happened. I didn't know how they'd react. My mom hugged me. "I'm so proud of you, Chloe," she said. That made me feel good.

Dad looked at me seriously. Was he disappointed in me

for quitting? Then a smile spread across his face. "That's my Chloe," he said. "That's my girl."

The next few days were a little strange. Kids still gathered around me and asked for my autograph, but I knew my days of fame were ending. Then on Saturday, I saw my name blasted across the front page of a gossip newspaper.

I was getting out of a cab at of the Calico agency when I saw the paper in the newsstand right out front. It said DIFFICULT CHLOE CHANG FIRED FROM TV SHOW. "Difficult!" I cried out loud as I stood by the stand. That was so unfair!

My eyes traveled over to the next bunch of papers. A slightly smaller headline in another one read TROUBLED TEEN BLOWS BIG RECORD DEAL! Dad had called Dave Davis and backed out of the recording contract. He said Mr. Davis was very nice about it. I didn't call *this* being very nice.

Suddenly I felt as if everyone on the street must be looking at me. I was so embarrassed! With tears in my eyes, I ran into the building and onto the elevator. Walking past the agency receptionist, I hurried straight to the Red Room. All I wanted to do was find someplace where I could hide from the world.

When I got into the Red Room, Nikki and Tracey were already there. The minute I entered, Nikki quickly folded up a newspaper she was reading. By the light of the red bulb, I could see it was a third paper that I hadn't yet seen. Without a word, I took the paper from her.

"It's page twenty-seven," she said glumly.

The headline of the story was CHLOE'S STRANGE BEHAVIOR PUZZLES FANS. It said my fans were brokenhearted that I'd decided to destroy my career on purpose. "They make me sound like some sort of nut," I moaned.

"We know why you did what you did," said Tracey.

"Thanks, but this kind of publicity might finish off my modeling career," I said. "No clients want a 'troubled teen' selling their products."

"But you're not a troubled teen," Nikki protested. "Everyone who knows you knows that."

"Not everyone knows me," I said, feeling awful. I'd been willing to give up acting and singing, but I'd been modeling nearly all my life. I didn't want to lose that. Even if I had only a few years of my career left, I wanted those years.

"Let's go see Ms. Calico," Nikki suggested.

"I don't know what she—" I began to object. I was cut off by Ashley, who rushed into the room.

"Kate wants you in her office," she told me.

All of us left the Red Room and headed toward Kate's office. Before we even got there, we met her in the hall. "Oh, there you are, Chloe," she said. "I called my friend Jessica Daniels, the editor of *Teen Life*. She's on her way here to do an exclusive interview with you. This is your chance to tell what really happened."

"I don't trust interviews," I said.

"Don't worry. You can trust Jessica," Kate said.

"Can we stay with her?" Ashley asked.

"Yes, of course," said Kate. "All of you, into my office."

"I'm supposed to be at a Little Princess catalog shoot in a half hour," I told Kate.

Kate smiled. "Well, then I guess you'll have to talk fast."

Chapter Fifteen

Two weeks later, I was once again the center of attention. But this time it wasn't for doing stunts, singing badly, or photographing well, or even for being a troubled teen. I was the first place winner of the District 12, junior high division, essay contest.

That's right. My essay about Grandma actually won first prize!

No one could have been more shocked than I was, but I was also delighted. My parents were thrilled! Grandma was, too. It was the first thing I'd done in a long time that really made me feel proud of myself.

Now my whole family sat in the front row of the auditorium of Harriet Tubman Junior High and waited to see me receive my trophy onstage, plus my fifty-dollar prize. I looked out from the wings of the stage and noticed three familiar faces sitting behind my family. Ashley, Nikki, and Tracey had come, too. I'd told them about the award, but I hadn't expected them to attend the ceremony. They're such great friends.

On the stage, the boy who'd won in the elementary school division took his trophy and walked off. Mrs. Elmont came on and began talking to the audience. "Our next award winner is someone who has many future career paths open to her," she said. "She is a multitalented girl, but I personally hope she'll choose writing as her vocation. Her essay, which she'll read for us now, proves she has a great gift for writing. Our first-place winner is Ms. Chloe Chang."

The audience clapped as I walked onstage. I heard a high-pitched whistle that I recognized as coming from my brother Matt. I smiled, imagining my father scowling at him for that. I saw Tracey, Nikki, and Ashley standing as they clapped wildly. Dad pounded his large hands together while Mom beamed beside him.

Once again I was filled with joy. The world seemed like a wonderful place. I was happy not only that I'd won, but that the people I loved were so happy for me.

These were people who knew who I really was. These were the people who mattered to me.

When I got to center stage, I was able to see Grandma clearly, sitting on the other side of Mom. I smiled at her, and she smiled back.

"My grandmother was a feminist before she ever heard the word," I began. The essay took over five minutes to read. As I spoke, I realized that it was good because of my writing, but also because Grandma's life was so inspiring. "The thing I admire so much about Grandma," I continued, reading the closing, "is that she has always lived her life with honor. In good times and bad times, Grandma has been true to the beliefs she held in her heart. When she was wealthy, she would not be defined by that narrow world, just as she wouldn't let herself be defined by poverty and hard times. She has walked through her life with her head high, always listening—listening to the needs of people around her, and listening to the teachings of her own heart. If I was granted just one wish, it would be to become even half the person my grandmother is."

At the end, when I lifted my head, I saw that Grandma was wiping tears from her eyes with a tissue. Seeing her cry got me all choked up, too. As everyone clapped, I looked at the ceiling to keep my tears from brimming over.

Mrs. Elmont walked out and handed me my trophy

and the check. "Chloe, did you find this essay difficult to write, or did it come to you easily?" she asked in front of everyone.

"It came pretty easily," I said. "It was one of the few things that seemed to have some meaning for me in these last few weeks, which have been a little on the strange side."

"We know you're a busy girl these days, but do you think you'd like to do any more writing?" she asked. "As I said, I think you have the talent to be a wonderful writer."

"I'd like to write more, yes. Maybe I will try to be a writer someday," I told her and the audience.

"That would be terrific," Mrs. Elmont said. She turned toward the audience and spoke into the microphone. "That concludes our ceremony. Thank you all for coming. And congratulations to all our talented young winners."

When I walked down off the stage, I ran over to where my parents were sitting. They all congratulated me. Then I got to Grandma. She held me tight and squeezed. I squeezed back. "This is the finest gift anyone has ever given me, Flower," she said.

"I love you," I said, holding on to her.

"I love you, too."

When we stopped hugging, I noticed Dad was standing nearby. "I thought we would all go to lunch over at Florio's," he said. "Many famous writers used to meet there. Invite your friends if you like."

"Okay, Dad, thanks," I said.

I hurried over to my friends and invited them to join us. They agreed to come. "Look what I have," Ashley said, taking something from her large handbag. "Kate sent this to Mom's fax machine this morning."

She handed me a black-and-white copy of an article entitled THE REAL CHLOE CHANG STEPS FORWARD. "It's an advance copy of *Teen Life*," Ashley explained. "It won't be on the stands until next week."

On the left-hand page of the article was a full-page picture of Ashley, Nikki, Tracey, and me sitting on Kate's office couch with our arms around one another. The caption beside it read *Chloe's model gal pals say she's the greatest.*

"Look at the part I underlined," Ashley pointed out, flipping the stapled pages over to the last page.

Model Ashley Taylor, a close friend, says she admires Chloe for standing up for what she thought was right. "Not a lot of people do that," Ashley said. "When you find someone who does, you know she's someone special."

I smiled at Ashley. "Thanks."

"Did you mean it about someday becoming a writer?" Nikki asked as we began walking up the aisle out of the auditorium.

"Maybe. I don't know," I said honestly. "I guess I'll just have to listen to my heart."